the way none of this happened

mike breiner

Fomite

Burlington, Vermont

ISBN-13: 978-1-937677-60-2
Library of Congress Control Number: 2013952787

Fomite
58 Peru Street
Burlington, VT 05401
www.fomitepress.com

for Linda and Birdie

"*...I think you're fine and soft and sacred.*" She looked up
from the page. "Was that a typo?"
"Was what a typo?"
"Sacred."
"Sacred?" She handed him the page. "Sacred."
"Did I say sacred?" He scribbled a note. "I meant scared.
You're fine and soft and scared."

*One afternoon, Walter Benjamin was sitting inside the Café Les
Deux Magots in Saint Germain des Prés when he was struck with
compelling force by the idea of drawing a diagram of his life, and
knew at the same moment exactly how it was to be done. He
drew the diagram, and with utterly typical ill-luck lost it again a
year or two later. The diagram, not surprisingly, was a labyrinth.*
—Terry Eagleton

*Many people mistake for original ideas what are merely coinci-
dences.* —Christa Wolf

*What if the "author" is no longer found at the origin of the
"text?" Every language awaits its author – you, I, anyone –who
will make fiction surge forth from it.*
—Jacques Ehrmann

*Why do they write at all? Because they are all failures, incapable
of summoning up lifelong disciplines and diligences for any other
vocation or discovering any sense in it. Writing is a problem of
organization. No writer should imagine that he invents anything
new. Everything that he feels, thinks, digs up, combines is only a
small part of what has already been felt, thought and experienced
by many others. He only arranges it in his way, produces a certain
summary that in the moment he produced it has already been
superseded by reality.*
—Gunther Herberger

*For the thing so overdone is from the purpose of playing, whose
end, both at the first and now, was and is, to hold, as it were, the
mirror to nature, to show virtue her own feature, scorn her own
image, and this very age and the body of the time his form and
pressure.*
—Hamlet 3, ii, 20-25

PREFACE

The moments are more interesting than the days…I just found
the poster announcing the events scheduled that Fall at the Vehicule Gallery. On line five I read "oct.16 Mike Breiner Tinker
Greene, Bill Davis, Marcia Goldberg." Google tells me that
there's a Sunday, Oct. 16, in 1977. So it's Sunday, October, 16,
1977, and the Vehicule Poets have invited some of the Poet's
Mimeo members up to Montreal, and Bill, Marcia, Tinker and
myself have just done a reading at the Vehicule Gallery on Ste.
Catherine St. We're someplace having a beer, and waiting for our
sandwiches. Tom Konyves, one of the Vehicule poets, comes up
to the table and says to me, "Nice reading. What was that last
piece?" I tell him it's the start of a prose project called "Stop Me
if You've Heard this one Before," and he leans down towards me
with a stern expression on his face and asks, "You read prose at
a poetry reading?" and just stares at me. I don't have an answer,
and I can't tell how serious his question is, so I raise my bottle
of Molson to my lips, and that's where this begins. From the
beginning, I've thought of public readings as my primary publication point. There have been a few appearances in print over
the years, especially when I was part of Poet's Mimeo, but for the
most part since Bill and I put together Boys Will be Boys in 1980,
I've been content with sharing work at readings, a curious trait I
share with many from the old Poet's Mimeo mob. Over the years
I've had many variations of that conversation with Tom. Someone might come up to me after a reading and say they enjoyed
my story or my poem when I might have read a poem or story. I

might or might not point out that that poem was in fact a story, or that story a poem, and that was where the matter ended. The story or poem was for all intents and purposes published, and then filed until next time. Occasionally someone might ask for a contribution to a magazine, or I might do some little edition on my own. A while back a bunch of us started a very occasional publication called Dogear after Bud Lawrence start talking about publication, and I started thinking about putting together a book. Before all that Marc and Donna had asked me if I'd like to send something to Fomite, so finally, after an extended period of fluctuation and self-criticism, I set to putting a manuscript together that became this collection of prose pieces. It contains aphorisms, prose poems, very short fiction, little essays, and more than a few rants that I've written and read over the past 40 years. The first entry is one of the earliest (and has been the first piece in the various manuscripts for a long time, and the final one is one of the latest, but beyond that there's nothing close to a chronological order. There's been a little tweaking and tightening of the texts (thanks for noticing, Marc), but I've tried to not do a lot of rewriting, although I've got to admit that it's been a struggle because the kid was a bit of a punk.

As I said earlier, I've thought about this manuscript off and on for a long time. A first run at it was called Lying with the Dead, and I did that for some literary contest in 1975. 20 pages or so, with alternating prose fragments and quotes from books I was reading at the time. It lost the contest and went into the file cabinet. The next time, the quotes were gone — they now reside in another folder that I've taken to calling From (my version of Tillie Olsen's Silences, I guess) —and that version was called, as I told Tom Konyves in 1978, Stop Me If You've Heard This One Before. The joke when I did readings from this version was that it was a purely rhetorical title, and should not be an invitation for audience participation. The poster for my first reading of that one (my first solo show) is a nice poster that Tinker put together. After that one went in the cabinet, I read the American anarchist Benjamin Tucker's Instead of a Book, and I used that title for a while, but in the 80's it became Always Already, a phrase that came up in my (mis)readings of contemporary French philosophy. I had a strong attachment to that title until this past summer. In August I did a little reading at Bailey Howe Library hoping I could use the event to wrap up the year's work on the manuscript I'd been doing. It didn't quite work out that way. I entitled my presentation The Way That None of this Happened, and as I've been finally wrapping this up, most folks seem to like that title better than Always Already.

I guess that's about it. I've got some suggestions for the best approach to this thing, but I think I've gone long enough. I'll just leave you to it. Thanks for reading. And listening. Be well.

— Mike, April 2013

I almost forgot. Sorry for any stray punctuation, misspellings or moments of raging syntax that remain in what follows. We'll fix them in the mix.

Writing about not writing is a terrible way to say you're not writing. Not not writing scares me. Not not writing can make me think i'm not writing. i'm not writing about not writing, which i'm not, but about not not writing, which i am. So i will. Maybe every day, and maybe not every day. But regardless of my writing, or not writing, or not not writing about writing or not writing, this is still an exercise where there is none, discipline where there is none, desire where there is none.

=-=

"Nothing is real" never meant less. Something old-fashioned, he thought. Call it suspense, mystery, the terminal. A terminal. A beach. A bus driving along the street-hard sand in pursuit of the retreating tide. Consider a campfire in the lobby of every major workplace with a large kettle of hot water suspended above it. "Women folk" tend the fire, and of course "Women folk" is only the job title for this position which is scheduled for all members of the workforce. Thus any sexism and its attendant stereotypes is merely a branding, not a practice. Living in a different world. The sunrise is just there, a luminescent layer lining the horizon. Turn your back and go down the stairs into another world. Can we dare to be like them, shouting poems into the air like rifles, without wondering or caring how or where they come back to earth? Finally (for now) — "We read, really, to find out what we already know," V.S. Naipul wrote. Which, of course, begs the question: why do we write? Clearly an uncertain process, especially for those committed to the creation (or is that man-ufacture?) of these blocks of prose.

-=-

FROM A KIND OF MOTION WE CALL HEAT

The spiritual disposition of a poet inclines to catastrophe
— Osip Mandelstam

Part 1. The last of a cardinal's song against the rising night. Or another way to start. Directly, or at least in a general sort of direction. The straightest line if not the shortest distance already alluded to. The book whose title I've appropriated for these lines is subtitled: a History of the Kinetic Theory of Gases in the Nineteenth Century. No, I haven't read it, and probably never will. Like Das Kapital or The Psychology of Dreams, or those 1200 page novels of Neal Stephenson that I keep buying. Like too many of the novels I've been starting in the past few years. To read that is, not to write. I've given up the idea of ever writing a novel. For better or worse, especially since I usually work in prose, I'm a miniaturist. Not only in composition, but in vision as well. That couple in the corner? Leave 'em alone. They've got their own lives to lead, even if you're one of them. But the line of sweat tracing his eye socket? That's me. The lazy ancient circumference of a glass' watermark on the table sitting between them? That's me. Then again…or there again.

The bright trails of bottle rockets vomited up into the night, or the slow trail of a hot air balloon along the river at sunrise. That conversation there, miles away, trapped behind a brace of headlights sliding from the horizon into the darkness of an evening's landscape. Yes, that again. Not much changes here at the window. A melody, a melodica, let's call it a melody on a melodica. And then a heavier reverb is dialed into this version, with the clatter of a typewriter, or the more muted tapping of the computer keyboard echoing against the sigh of the ceiling fan and blending into a rhythm anchoring however lightly the swirl of the synthesizer's tune. "Lotta people gonna go hungry tonight," Joe Strummer sings another time. The kind of motion we call heat. It's another world to be sure, but somebody else will have to tell you the tale of the intrepid ancient's circumnavigation of the circumference of that watermark. "The reality of capitulation comes naturally to those intent on self-examination," Huston Paschal wrote somewhere. Confessions out of nowhere. Or revelations, maybe. Breathless. You know, like the movie.

-=-

Downstairs, he hears the dog barking, then laughter and voices. He turns away from the door and looks down at the notebook he had been writing in before being distracted. He is desperate to be working again, anything for an excuse to be left alone, but he already knows how the rest of the day will go. She will be upstairs soon, there, at the door and letting him know who has arrived. His friends, or hers, it will make no difference. He doesn't want to go downstairs. He is almost as repulsed by the idea of going downstairs as he is by the thought of himself staying here to work, or his work itself, even at the same time that he feels the need to finish filling this page he has been writing on. Back to that again. Caring so much for the writing that he looks for any excuse not to finish it. He tries to fill the page with this thought but it is past him too fast, an object before he has the opportunity to make it his own and preserve it on the page. It's gone and he is alone, and downstairs the dog is finally quiet, and he can hear voices calling his name. He hears the familiar footsteps on the stairs. He turns back to the door, and with pen poised over paper, assumes a look of irritation.

=-=

DERIVE

the (a) long howl across the night. A passing car. Words (if there are any) are lost in the motion of recording them long before any meaning evolves. If this has a someplace, he & Linda might be there. It might be late in the fall. they might be hand in hand. They are hand in hand. The path they are walking runs the rim of a point of land that is jutting into the ocean. Beaches dot its shore. They are watching the ocean, the sky, the motion of a cluster of seabirds across the bay. They come around a corner of the path and look down a clutter of rocks that spills down to the water's edge. Another sense of motion is discerned when geysers of spray erupt between the rocks as waves work their way into this description of a landscape. Sheathes of ice coat some of the rocks between them and the waves. And later, after this tableau has been passed and they've finished their walk and are standing on the terrace outside their room, on the horizon he & Linda will see the glow of cities at night as with darkness what was sensed as easterly suddenly becomes southerly.

=-=

Or maybe to look for stories the way we look for rain — out the window, in puddles, signs of movement, contact. Is that how they do it, how we do it, the poets, the novelists, the writers? Find these stories that hold us just so. Find these characters that we will listen to for hours. A torrent of situations, cascading into heaps of paper, boxes, situations.

-=-

THE PROBLEM OF EMPTINESS

A forlorn diligence. The line of empty bottles on a window casing. There is the initial satisfaction of denial, a discussion of continuity. The lines must be ended. A little forgotten story about the future. It is either winter or summer. A case of extremes. No frost. No window at the top of the stairs. No seasonal view of the horizon. No one sitting there and watching the mountains catch the late light of summer. Or is it the sharp dead glare of winter? There are not even stairs.

=-=

A friend measures a work only by its success, and I fear that I've come to only measure a work by its failure.

-=-

Moods change like skies over the lake... You put down the pen and stare at what you've just written. You want to take a minute to explain, to clarify the point you're trying to make when suddenly the wind picks up, clouds appear, and first raindrops start hitting the window. Suddenly the clouds open, it starts pissing down rain, the door is open and everything is soaked. The rest of the afternoon is spent mopping, wringing and sponging, and nothing gets done. The entry is forgotten. The life that gets in the way of the living of it. In the field beyond the window, a tree is struck by lightning and killed. One afternoon it falls over, bringing down a stretch of fence when it falls. Your neighbor's cows get free, and graze along your driveway. You help round them up; the tree is pulled free from the fence and the branches are trimmed and piled. The fence is repaired. What's left of the tree trunk is suddenly a log left at the edge of the pasture. Insects flourish. In the middle of an afternoon next summer you sit on the log and finish this entry in you notebook. So what "just happens?"

=-=

Another of those dull moments. Another of those dull predictable moments. Irene points a gun at her head. Well, not really pointing. Irene is holding a gun to her head. Or Ira. Ira is holding a gun to his head. We can't be sure yet. Maybe Ira is holding a gun to Irene's head. Even Irene holding a gun to Ira's head. We just can't be sure. Like a shadow on a shade. A silhouette on a shade. 2 silhouettes on a shade. Overseen, as in overheard.

-=-

I'm a polyglot illiterate. I can't read in thousands of languages.

=-=

In the homestretch, as it were, in the last few pages of this notebook. I've been paging back through entries, finding the common threads. Today's date is 11/22/91. 28 years on from the JFK shooting. Another day the world changed. The start of another struggle. Another time. For now I've got a handful of poems under construction, some kind of a satire for work. I'm reading Breaking Bread, a book of dialogues between bell hooks and Cornel West on Black intellectual life. As I sit here on the edge of what seems to be an increasingly ego-driven, process-centered bureaucracy and culture and try to do critical analysis, i realize that it is ego-driven, process-centered art that mostly appeals to me. I sense a need to apply a critique to what I've been doing these past months. Or is that we? As I'm writing this I'm doing a public service shift in the Reference Department at the ARC desk. That's the Automated Resource Center desk. I'm surrounded by computer terminals accessing all sorts of databases. My primary responsibility for this desk shift is to help orient students and other patrons to using these databases for their research. As I write this passage most of the machines are not being used, and I'm ruminating on the largest contradiction of my shift: how can all of this information be generating so much passivity and, I don't know, something like stupidity? How in spite of the contradictions of what we know and can know is it that the system is able to continue this downward spiral? But maybe if I could get out of this art ghetto I like to envision myself in, perhaps things might be different. Who knows? Time for that new notebook, See you soon…

-=-

The river of syntax or the forest of syntax or the vale of syntax or the swamp of syntax.

=-=

IMPETUS
— for Bud Lawrence

If there's no earth, invent one, if the earth doesn't go fast enough, leave it behind, take off, if there's no road, make one, invent it with feet, hands, arms, passion, necessity.
— Helene Cixous

Like you might say, Bud, I'll just toss it all out here. This morning on the way to work Charles Olson was reading to me in a lecture that was recorded in 1969, & I was listening to him in that half-hearing/half-listening first encounter kind of way as I walked the (or that) walk to work I've talked about before. Maybe if—let's be honest—when I read this I should read one of those other walking to work poems I've got to give you an idea of what this walk to work can do, but for now, as I start this, I mean really start to say what I was wanting to say to you, I'll tell you I'm at work here at the library, and I was upstairs looking for a copy of the Maximus Poems but instead I pulled down a copy of Archeologist of Morning & opened to For Sappho, Back, which is a nice link to my ongoing wonder at women's voices and a nice segue to another digression: it's a few weeks after I started writing this poem (and it was a poem when I started this revision) and I was to talking to Patty and she asked what I was reading and I said I was reading some Caribbean women writers and it seemed like they were changing my voice and with a laugh she asked if I thought this was some kind of puberty? But that's got nothing to do with the book I want to mention now, which is called Women's Voices and is a collection of essays about French feminists which is a long ways from Maximus which when I finally found a copy of I found the last poem that Olson had read to me as I went through the mechanical room on my way into the library in a nice allegorical recreation of this initiatory passage, reading to me in that old man/Massachusetts-coast tinged voice : tesserae / commisure – and I looked up from the poem and opened this notebook to scribble — "voices voiced / or indicated." And so, Bud, here we are with Butterick still unconsulted as we align this next bit wherein in one story a Jamaican women tells the story of a peeled orange, and in another an English woman peels an orange in a single delicate spiral, and in another, an American woman describes biting into crackly-skinned segments of juicy orange that she left sitting on a radiator, while another, Josephina Vicens, writes in her Empty Book: "… and the only thing that I express honestly is that what I wish I could write is either already written in the books that move me or will be written by other men in notebooks that won't resemble mine in any way, that won't be so pathetically full, this one of impotence, and the other one of blank, useless writing," and here by the computer back home where I type sits a photo of two boys in the Surinam rainforest, staring at me through masks made of large strips of what I wish could say was orange peel, and all this is sitting here in this paragraph (or maybe this poem) and waiting for something like transubstantiation, or some simpler suddenly recalled experiment in a beginner's chemistry set in an early 1960's kitchen, the one with sodium hydroxide, water, and phenolphthalein, water to wine and back. Nothing mysterious, just something we're able to do.

-=-

it was the time when CV's ruled the land. If awards & meetings mattered, neither would be necessary. Something fell in the next room, its clatter silencing the discussion. Check the door … close the window … carry on … a knowing smile, a nod. Noted and duly recorded, the meeting can continue.

=-=

Oswald's self-aggrandizing ego.

He never had a chance. It was like being called Adolf or Hein-rich and living in Germany in 1946. You kids out there think Saddam, or Osama. Call me Sam.

-=-

Articulated marginalia

The way of the world is stupid and obscure and must be so to fit man's intelligence.
-William Carlos Williams

How else to explain the need to share what I have discovered while rereading my copy of WCW's Imaginations? At the top of the final blank endpaper there is a bit of handwriting. It is written in my very boyish cursive style and reads — "Reading Paterson from the window." What exactly was that young fellow trying to say? As there's no context to attach to these five words, perhaps we can best parse out what he is trying to say by trying to imagine what he was getting ready to describe. Perhaps he was beginning a response to a mist-smothered morning as it was traversed by the sound of geese crossing above him out of sight. Or perhaps it was writ-ten on a winter's night sitting at a picture window in South Hero, a light from his neighbor's driveway beaming across a pasture slowly filling with new snow. Finally there is the lit-eral. Perhaps our young writer was actually reading Paterson

17

from the window using a podium suspended away from the house with some kind of articulated page turning apparatus in place. Or we can imagine him giving directions to a friend holding up the book for him on a roof, or the porch that may extend beyond the window at which he is sitting. Who can say for sure? It would seem we're standing at a fork in our storytelling road. Shall we continue on the uncertain path of the autobiographical, or start over and perhaps take the other path and avoid all of this speculation with a healthy dose of fiction? The fictioneer I aspire to be might like the possibilities to be explored in the image of a fledging poet inscribing this note in a book, but the autobiographer I am knows our young fellow only completely read Williams' major work in the past winter, some 40 years after the writing of these words. Where to go…where to go? In the meantime, it's another morning, another book, and again he begins to write – The mist lifts on another morning / The rose bush sways brownly above a smattering of green fists in the garden / & i irrationally long for the times of William the Silent — …and implications for further discussion become no clearer as I recall a cartoon Susan sent me in which a simple figure standing in a simple landscape advices the viewer to "Never give up on your stupid, stupid dreams."

=-=

Shards of stories, failed fables of alliteration. The dead pan expression of l'ecrivain. He leafs through the beginnings piled in front of him, a staggering collection of fits and starts, a tribute to a true lack of discipline. The warming television bursts into song, then the canned laughter of a situation comedy. He smiles, thinking of friends who lack his willfulness to leave behind a calling, even if only for a time. The son on the screen who gives up the priesthood for a tumble with the barmaid in a montage of shocked aunts and uncles scurrying about the countryside, disbelieving shakes of the head at uncomprehending telephone receivers, a grandmother crying before her crucifix in Innisfree. Eva Gabor is smiling from the corner of the living room, holding an ashtray shaped like a human head wearing a crown. "But Dahling," she says portraying Lisa Douglas, a relocated city gal on the situation comedy Green Acres, who has accompanied her dufus husband, a dissatisfied New York City attorney (Eddie Albert) to a wacky rural utopia called Hooterville. "But Dahling, people love to put their cigarettes out in the king's mouth." Another set of shrieks cut off as he changes the channel, and drops the page onto the pile, remembering what Bugs Bunny told him last weekend. "Conventions sure ain't what they used to be." He reaches for his notebook as he keeps changing the channel.

-=-

Listening to a gamelan with Claude Debussy at the Paris World Exposition of 1889

It's Friday, February 21, 1997 and I'm at work, and it's lunchtime. I'm writing a notebook entry recording some thoughts about the section in David Toop's book The Ocean of Sound where he's talking about Debussy's encounter with a gamelan at the 1889 Paris World Exposition and calling it one of the turning points in Western music, and I'm realizing that I'm not going to be able to pick Claude out of the crowd unless I run upstairs and take a peek at an illustrated biography of the man. I'll be right back. Okay. I'm just about ready to relate my encounter with Claude Debussy right after he first heard gamelan music at the 1889 Paris World Exposition. But before I do that let me tell you that it's also some time in the late 1970's and I'm about to hear gamelan music for the first time. And that's all you need to know as the needle on my old RCA automatic turntable comes down on Side One of Golden Rain, a record from that wonderful Explorer series that Nonesuch did back in the '60's. I'm in the living room of the apartment Linda and I were renting from Fred Reus up in South Hero in 1978. And maybe I'm lying on the couch and Ebony is curled up beside me, or maybe I'm standing at the window looking out across the fields and down toward the lake and I'm hearing this music that is just ... I don't know. Different. A first flurry of metallic clamor, then silence, then a response, and again, and a shorter silence and again, and again, until finally the entire ensemble is hammering its way into the room. There will be more encounters arising out of the playing of this record and no, I don't know why I bought it, except that it was probably selling for a buck someplace and I grabbed it. While I'm here I should tell you that the other side of Golden Rain is a recording of a performance of communal chanting called Ketjak, which will eventually lead me to picking up Ron Silliman's poem entitled Ket-jak, which in turn leads to a flirtation that has never really stopped with the school of Language poetry, but that, as they say, is another story. Later on there's an evening of wayang (Javanese shadow puppetry) with accompaniment provided by the Wesleyan Gamelan that I will attend with Max and Bill, an amazing night that is the model for a dream performance you also won't hear about now. Finally, there's a performance by a Balinese dance and music troupe that I saw at the Flynn Theater with Linda. It is these moments of first encounter that David Toop wants me to remember and try to relate to you as I stand there in each of those moments and sit here writing this description of me standing here waiting to exchange opinions with Claude Debussy at the 1889 Paris World Exposition. As the record ends in South Hero, as I read Ron Silliman's Language anthology In the American Tree in 1988, as I circle the gamelan in the First Congregational Church in 1980-some and also hold Linda's hand sitting in a 1993 Flynn Theater audience, I recognize Claude Debussy in the crowd exiting the pavilion (if there is a crowd exiting the pavilion, if in fact there is even a pavilion). I introduce myself to Claude Debussy, and after a several minutes of spirited discussion about the experience we've just shared, I suggest going somewhere for a coffee or perhaps a glass of wine. We find a table in a little outdoor cafe on the main boulevard of the 1889 Paris World Exposition (again, if there is a little outdoor cafe there on the main boulevard of the 1889 Paris World Exposition, if indeed if there is even a main boulevard of the 1889 Paris World

Exposition), order wine and continue our conversation. Paul Verlaine might pass our table, exchange salutations and join us. After a while, perhaps fortified by a second (or maybe it's the third) glass of wine I might read to Claude Debussy and Paul Verlaine what I've just written here on February 22, 1997 as I've transferred my notebook entry from the previous day to the computer, and perhaps we might discuss there at a little table in an outdoor cafe on the main boulevard of the 1889 Paris World Exposition how it is that writers can often remind us through their words of the richness of their experiences and imagination with these languages we share and how truly occasional it is that those words can be transformed into something like poetry.

-=-

Screenplay

The plot could be as simple as, "It's like he's Arjuna going out for cigarettes or a quart of milk."

=-=

Exaggeration is a question of where, when and how much. Like so many rhetorical devices still in use in these enlightened (or is that empowered?) times. Or maybe that's appropriated time. You read in a book ..."a diamond as big as a rat." You like that combination of words but maybe you'll enhance it. "A diamond as big as a fucking rat" in homage to the punch line of a great joke from your youth. Or maybe instead you use exaggeration. "A diamond as big as a rat and the rat is as big as a cat." A simple rhyming extension of an enlarging exaggeration. And then a nice absurdity. "A diamond as big as a rat as big as a cat as big as a school bus.". Then something topical, and by the time you record the digression you've got "a diamond as big as a rat as big as a cat as big as a school bus the size of the World Trade Center," and that's a lot kids moving past your kitchen window in an endless yellow bus as you pour another cup of coffee and watch the cloud of debris sliding down the street after it.

=-=

if the war doesn't come we're not victors, but alarmists.

-=-

BLUE SCRAPBOOK 8/17/77

Stock summer morning. Pots of coffee. Odd eggs. Toast. Juice. Okay, some donuts someplace. Kids hunched over bowls of cereal. Holidays winding down, or just another work day. Newspapers spread across tables, picking up stains, corners of coffee, of jam. Over it all radios turned on with disc jockeys offering melodies, reminiscences, forgiving the handshake with Nixon, avoiding the one we'll later call the fat Elvis. Love Me Tender comes on and breakfast tables give way to an explosion of front seats and backseats and movie theater seats and couches and beds and beach blankets and backyards and forest glades and rest areas and anatomies.

Thighs remembered, breasts under sweaters, under bathing suits, sleeveless blouses, under bras, a universe of fabrics. A galaxy of cocks, constellations of nipples. You Ain't Nothin' But a Hound Dog under suns, moons, underpants, denims, blue suede shoes, Chuck Taylors, corduroys. Then going to work. Buses, cars, occupants covetously staring at kids on vacation. In cities, in towns, in parks, by lakes and recalled. In 1966, I … in1962, I…In August 1958…in June 1970…Blue Hawaii, Roustabout, Kid Galahad, a filmography of starlets and lip-synching in a life time of drive-ins and steaming double features. On the front page. On the radio. Heartbreak Hotel, blue balls on the drive home. "I remember it like it was yesterday." A 1968 sunrise and beating off while looking across this continent of early morning situations, It's Now or Never. A world of variables. Of sock hops. Of proms. Of auditoriums and dance halls. Of America and Jailhouse Rock. Of Love Me Tender again. Of goodnights kisses and those intense tentative fucks. Of Elvis. The King is Dead. Long Live the King.

=-=

from A Kind of Motion We Call Heat
Part. 3. Amongst the parameters, someone suggests a point of clarification. Perhaps it might have been better to have started back there someplace, or maybe further on ahead a bit, but since we're here, we'll go on. But understand, here is not quite fiction, where all is but a ramshackle of vocabulary and tenses, so we'll endeavor to simply remain a calmer

accompaniment, and perhaps inevitably, a counterpoint to any emotions that might appear. An avalanche of lost moments, of squandered opportunities that equivocate desire. The phone rings in the late afternoon, an old joke about voices from the past is deflected. "No," someone is saying, "it's just a different voice coming from a different now that's occurring down the river a ways." Later this might be pulled away as debris, detritus that inhabits the paragraph's progress, or not. Eventually, a line for another more well-defined character. All for this concept called forward, or maybe it is just a sense of motion. Something to do with current. Discovery. Fact-checking a history. Finding a new lie, a new context, a part of the routine. When memory is presented as the waste of experience.

-=-

Word leaks out
or
words
leak
out

another misplaced letter and a bill is past due
or a thank you delayed becomes an affront

the lost life as a window becomes a door
an apocryphal moment described becoming ephemeral in the
retelling

or what to do if the trap fades before the cascade of electronic
babble
to be replaced by the smaller intensity of hand drums and
bells
the clearing becoming clarified as an unfettered frustration
becomes a lingering
an adjoining of these 2 desperate moments conjoined to a
disparate third

the pulled plug's resultant silence is "wonderfully inevitable"

The things that cannot be made up anymore. Another deriv-
ative found on the path tracking away from an utterance like
"nothing in this novel is pure invention." Fiction can once
again be put in quotes. Or the quotidian. Another example
of applied misreading. Something stops you. The pen, say,
doesn't take to the notebook page and a first word drifts off
as the ink ceases to flow. You stop writing. The pen works on
another page. You return to the original where the pen again
stops and the empty page wins out and remains as another
page is tested, then used as your thoughts are recorded. And
transformed. The still empty page taunts you as you discover
something is amiss. It is suddenly impossible to stem your
thoughts. Images are not quite right as lines lengthen and the
text begins to take shape. Your text is rolling down the page
and on to the next, relentlessly, as suddenly the original reason for beginning gives way to another. Or a revision as this
is copied over and carried on. The way wind enters a wintry

evening as you look up from book or music, and reaching for a pen, sense motion in the window and acknowledging the silence of the empty chair give in to the urge to "get it right," to "make it real." A landscape to be filled at the sound of a voice. And the need to discern a difference, the difference. The running line not being unlike the running of the water. The way both might fall steadily. A sense of gravity lost in self-consciousness as automatic writing is confused with sustained writing. As word leaks out, or words leak out.

=-=

A simple attention getter. What to say, how to say it. A way to work music into my silence. A guileless quiet introduction to the evening's proceedings.

-=-

Another wonderful weekend of booksale-ing. The year in review w/ Jay — Bow gossip, families, friends, the world, the work. The question—Jay asks if i'm happy in my role as an unpublished crank. i answer very. Conversation with John B.'s wife Lisa. we jump miles as friends — it seems — when i admit i've forgotten her name as we poke through piles of kid books at the Williamstown sale. At lunch she tells us about her writing, a non-fiction work on a North Carolina mid-wife, and the workshop she's taking this summer in Paris with Philip Lopate. The next morning in Hanover standing in the rain in the pre-sale line she asks me about my writing. The crank plays the Poet's Mimeo tape and runs through the projects — Domesticities, Always Already, the bibliography, the poems. It's always an impressive edifice, this unfinished body of work, and the crank wonders aloud if a Phillip Lopate workshop might help, but then recalls he unfortunately won't be in Paris this summer. Lisa smiles and says she's been working on her book for nine years. The crank smiles and nods, the doors open and the line starts to move. As a last question, she asks me to describe my style, and of course the crank can't answer. Anyway, it's great fun to be taken seriously. Later, as we wait to cash out, going through Jay's score, i can finally answer Lisa's question as i come across a copy of Barthes by Barthes. i flip through it and say to Jay, "this is what i write like ... without the intellect of course." Jay takes the book from my hands and offers his version of the Giaconda smile. Movies watched in two nights—Third Man and Medium Cool, as well as parts of Dead Men Don't Wear Plaid, Twilight of the Ice Nymphs, and tape one of Peter Watkins's La Commune.

-=-

Draining a last majito. Tonguing loose a bit of mint hanging between your teeth while in a lovely retro bright green metal (aluminum?) glass you swirl the dregs of ice and rum and sugar into one last swallow to chase that burst of mint across your tongue, one last cold gulp against the heat in the kitchen where you're all hiding from the swarming mosquitoes in the backyard, all the while staring at a mayfly spending who knows how much of its life cycle perched on Anna's sleeve even as she describes its life cycle to someone i can't recall, maybe Susan, maybe Sara, and maybe most its life if once we go out on the porch and she brushes it off into the evening and a bird grabs it, or maybe she brushes too hard or maybe it's already mated and ready to end its day on earth if a mayfly has access to anything like a sense of existential languor and i'm guessing it doesn't since it is a mayfly and probably more interested in mating or eating or just plain living than pondering its by our standards brief stay here on the orb and the ice bucket is empty and only a quarter inch of rum sits in the oversized bottle there on the counter. As we go outdoors, Anna brushes at her sleeve and sends the mayfly out into the heat of the evening, and you take a Harp out of the refrigerator, open it, and follow outside to the party.

=-=

Note during the first time listen to Havergal Brian's Sympho-
ny #3 — find bio. Coal miner's son, ends up as clerk in London. 20+ symphonies written after age 50. Liner notes imply
almost nothing heard during lifetime. Sounds familiar. Oh, &
a Mandelstam quote (courtesy Guy Maddin's Journals?) —
"It is terrifying to think that our life is a tale without a plot or
a hero, made up out of desolation and glass, out of the fever-
ish babble of constant digression." i guess it's a synchronous
moment as the next line in my notebook reads ... "end of the
record." On to side 2.

=-=

"I knew things had changed, that i had changed, that first
day i drove past a body and didn't even slow down." A great
first sentence. with all it implies. How many days did i stop?
How many days did i slow down? And how did it take me
five sentences to ask why there are bodies lying in the street?
And why is it that you still don't know?

-=-

THE DREAMS
1.
i'm sleeping in Richmond, Virginia on the night of the first
dream, and we're in a room that i don't recognize. A dormi-
tory, or maybe a hotel room. A temporary lodging for people

in transit. We are my mother, my sisters, my father, myself.
We're all younger. Dad has the longish still black hair of his
40's, the culture's late 60's or early 70's. And that posits this
room as someplace remembered in Terre Haute, Indiana or
Erie, Pennsylvania, and that means this dream is some kind of
simulation of the trip the family took to Kansas in the weeks
that bracketed Woodstock, the first Woodstock in 1969. But
for me it's now. My reactions are coming from a 47 year old
me and i know that Pop is dead and that this is a dream and
that everyone else in the room is older whenever they open
their mouths and that what's happening is now and they're
having the "what are we going to eat" conversation and Pop
turns to me and asks what i feel like and i shrug like i always
did which is my best recollection of my version of the sullen
teen syndrome and he smiles and mutters "Useless" which is
what will be the last thing my father will say to me before he
goes into the coma. It was like this: i was helping Mom get
him out of bed to get him to the commode and he was so frail
i didn't want to squeeze and i was being so gentle i couldn't
keep my grip and i almost dropped him and he looked right at
me and said, "Useless." in this so soft whisper. So in the hotel
room in Terre Haute, Indiana or maybe Erie, Pennsylvania,
the guy calls his slouching sun useless and dismisses him with
a wave of a windbreaker that he picks up off the bed. And
Pop turns back to the conversation with my mother and my
sisters and i stand up and head for the door. In the other room
my sister JoAnne is sitting at a writing desk in a room that
is clearly someplace else, maybe one of the apartments she's

lived in since 1969. i'm only certain that this room is not in the hotel where she and Kay and Mom are talking with Pop about supper. I ask her, "Are you doing this?" nodding back into the hotel room and she shrugs in acknowledgement. i ask her how she did it because i hadn't seen Pop in a dream since he died 6 months ago. She says she doesn't know how but it works, and keeps writing so i go back to the hotel room and it's empty and i go to the window and see the five of us in the parking lot standing around that old green Plymouth Fury we made that trip in. We all keep looking at the door to this room and even i look impatient standing down there in that parking lot in Terre Haute, Indiana or Erie Pennsylvania and i know i'm not going to leave this room and i'm not going to talk to Pop again until next time i can remember a dream that he's in and i wake up and i'm in Dawn and David's guest room in Richmond, Virginia and it's October 2000 and i'm looking for my pen so that i can write this down.

2.

11/28/02

Getting the paper this morning i found a thin layer of snow covering everything and thought, "Pop had been partly right," and thinking that starts the recollection. Dream light, dream time, dream locale. A post-storm light with no sun and the snow belt high, belly high across what looks like the UVM Green, a fresh and untouched white even here at the edge of the car width wide plowed path that might be South Prospect Street i'm walking on heading north to what might be Pearl Street, where the street widens as it traverse down a hill towards the city. Call it a city, as it seems to be more like a version of Burlington than Burlington itself. As i move out onto the wider path i look up from my feet and see Pop driving past in his 1965 Plymouth Satellite. Because of the conditions he's driving slow, then slower as he sees my wave, coming to a stop down the hill a little ways. i run to the car, open the passenger door and jump in. Pop is wearing one of his old summer uniforms, pale blue short-sleeve shirt and lightweight blue-gray pants. His hair is longish in back, black curls from the trendy 70s. Looking out the window at the snow i say, "i'm glad this is just a dream," and he looks over at me. "Are you sure about that?" He's got me. i sit back and notice the bundle of magazines between us on the bench seat (which the Satellite didn't have i note as i'm writing this down) It's bound with one of those leather straps with the intricate little metal clasp thingee that i always remember lying around the house when I was growing up. They made great tourniquets when war games drew blood and needed triage. Pop looks young and healthy and happy and, i suddenly realize, not that much older than me.

"So what's it like?" i finally ask. The look he gives me is long, like it's a scene in a movie. So long i want to tell him to keep his eye on the road. Finally he smiles. "It's pretty nice. We have lobster all the time. It's really too bad that i never cared for lobster." i laugh and look out the window and the snow is gone as the car sits at a red light. We're a block from

Church Street where i know he's going to drop me off and i
can't figure out how to say goodbye so i ask him how he got
here. The answer is more than a little vague and confusing,
not helped by the fact that his voice seems to be fading away.
Something about a charm, an old woman from a book he
motions to that is sitting under the bundle of magazines. Its
cover is a dark brown, almost black with faded letters em-
bossed on the cover. i look up from the book to ask him the
author's name and i'm sitting in a booth in a diner i don't recognize and Jim McGinniss is sitting opposite me and asking,
"Who's Roycroft?" and i'm standing up and heading for the
bathroom, thinking about the front seat of a Plymouth Satellite and the warmth of Pop's bare arm through the sleeve of
my parka. "Fucking dreams," i mutter as i wave for another
cup of coffee.

-=-

An afternoon of situations, an accumulation of regrets, re-
trievals, recriminations. A traffic jam, a perfect pearl of irritation, the day brought to a perfect close, & so close to the exit,
to sit & watch the day go by, inch by inch.

=-=

REAL LIFE PALES IN COMPARISON

This is not real. A five year old, his back burned red as the
Budweiser sun hat that he's wearing, is running up and down
the beach, jumping beach towels along the water's edge. Just

when you thought it was safe to go back in the water there's all this yelling, as this guy, a plastic shark fin strapped to his back, pops out of the lake, gasping laughter into the face of his victim, even as some critic yells from the beach, "It's fresh water, you fucking moron," as a radio is turned up, and asshole DJ interrogations stumble across the sand.

"Hot enuf foryah?"

"Cat's meltin' on the sidewalk, daddyo. Gotta request."

"Name it, kiddo."

'Wanna hear Holidays in the Sun, daddyo."

"And who's that for, kiddo?"

"Everybody at the beach, daddyo," and this cheer goes up here on our utopian beach, as after the sound of marching feet and someone muttering "a cheap holiday in other people's misery" pushes out of a chorus of radios, there's that stuttering guitar introduction and there's Johnny Rotten singing, "I don't wanna holiday in the sun," spilling across all those burned backs and pale sacrosanct bellies. A couple of guys are sitting on a log that washed up on the beach in the spring, sipping from wide mouthed bottles of Piel's Real Draft, and one of them points at a kid standing at the edge of the water peeing and chuckles, "Manneken Pis," as further out in the water two kids are standing with that look that says "I'm pissing in the lake and you don't know it" as they wave to their parents, and between them there's an older guy standing waist deep in the lake, finishing his lunch, half a burger in two bites, ready to dive at the last gulp and smack of mustardy lips. His wife yells from an oversized Pepperidge

Farm Goldfish beach towel she's sitting on something about waiting 20 minutes, her legs going red as she's sits there thinking about lifeguards, about summer nights and remembered or imaginary back seats and drive-ins, and she never thinks I'm wet for you, daddy, as "I wanna go to the new Belsen" slides over lotion slopping down a back, and cocoa butter warming along a shoulder, and a belch, and a giggle, and, and this young thing just runs by bouncing around in a green Speedo and the two guys lower their beers and laugh and dig elbows into each other's sides and one yells to her, "Hey lady," and she stops just beyond them, just sort of breathing and waiting and sure of herself as she turns to these two turkeys sitting on this log and smiling up at her, and the other one says, "We're members of the Olympic Selection Committee and we were wondering if you wouldn't mind just sort of running back and forth in front of us for a while," and the sun sort of sits high above the water as they laugh at that tight green sheathed ass bounding off into the afternoon, and on the radio someone is asking for the same song all over again, and no one can remember the last time they heard a Sex Pistols song get repeated on the radio, and there's a giggle in the bushes up by the road and this woman is playing with her three little children at the edge of the water, and it's raining at Fenway and nobody cares because out in the water a young woman is falling out of her bathing suit and "doing it very well" a guy says, his wife looking away, her hand brushing along his thigh, and marijuana smoke wafts across the tableau, mixing with the smell of hotdogs and hamburgs on a grill someplace down the beach, and I – yeah…I'm here…I'm one of these characters – I want to say that real life pale in comparison, but Johnny Rotten drowns me out snarling, "I don't understand this bit at all," and I look up and see an airplane way up high, its exhaust plume going to silver and white above us, and yeah, I'm giving in to cheap conventions now. That contrail is a thread going out across the sky joining us to another beach, another day, and another beach, and another day, and another, and another, into a string of beaches running across the land, becoming a single day and a single land-like beach where a string of nice little girls and boys are looking at nice people smoking nice marijuana cigarettes and eating nice hot dogs covered with nice mustard, listening to nice baseball games or nice records being played by nice people working for nice radio stations watched over by nice regulation agencies, and none of us nice people are at this nice beach on this nice day. We're sitting at even another beach. Call it Third Beach. And it's the Fourth of July, and this other beach we're on is big as all outdoors. It's an All-American beach three thousand miles long. And there's not a single piece of glass on this beach to cut your foot open on, and there's not a single sharp pointy stone, there's only movieland boulders scattered across the clean white sand waiting for kids to play on, or real lovers to sit in their shade holding hands and maybe kissing on the sly. It's an all-American beach where everyone has an even Coppertone tan, and all of the radios are playing the same song, and it's not Holidays in the Sun because nobody's even heard of Holidays in the Sun on this real beach, Third Beach, where they sing along in the throes of disco fever. The sea sloshes in to the disco beat, or maybe occasionally crashes in with a country music conniption and when the songs end the waves always fill the silence. It's a nice all-American kind of ending where all the little voices are flowing together, accommodating, not like the cacophony back at the beginning of these sentences. And when all of the accommodating voices start blending together, it gets so quiet. All the chicks. All the dudes. All the moms and dads. And then there's the girl who got acid thrown in her face because she tried to look like Farrah and did it too good, and pissed off somebody. This really happened in one of those redneck states with an Indian name. She's all smiles one afternoon, her blond hair wavy and tumbling like and then it's sizzling in the lockers, stinking and melting as she screams. But that's then and this is now, and it's summer, the Fourth of July, and she's out on Third Beach tanning those great legs, her new haircut and scars covered by a big floppy beach hat. And now she's watching this '72 Vega pulling into the parking lot across the road, its muffler hanging by a piece of twisted up hanger, its radio blaring something different into the afternoon and garnering stares from all the nice people, running off this story and shrinking the beach back down to something I can handle so I can finish this, and now she's watching three guys tumble out of the car, then three girls, and one of them sees her watching them, and waves to the girl in the big floppy beach hat sitting by herself, and our girl is that girl waving back to her friends, pulling off her hat so that her wave becomes that much brighter, that much bigger, and suddenly it's like a fairy tale the way she's feeling, watching her friends race across the road and onto the beach, the scars on her face and shoulders melting away as the music from the Vega and the boom boxes carried on the boys' shoulders fill the wave-filled not quite silence of Third Beach, and she can feel her face flushing as her friends get nearer. And all of the nice people sitting around the girl, the quiet girl who hadn't bothered anyone all summer, wondered as they sat on their Star Wars beach towels and their Budweiser Nascar beach towels and their Saturday Night Fever beach towels and their Disneyland beach towels, they wondered where that quiet girl they'd sat with all summer here on Third Beach could have found such boisterous friends, and now none of them can recognize the young woman who is greeting her friends as they drop to the beach around her, slapping the sand in time to the beat of This Year's Girl.

-=-

Or again – at work and cataloging the book State Failure, Collapse & Reconstruction, edited by Jennifer Milliken and published by Blackwell in 2003, and misreading the title of James Boyce's chapter, Aid conditionality as a tool for Peace building, as Air conditionality as a tool for Peace building, and wondering what would help negotiations more: money or comfort?

=-=

i'm thinking: i'll write about this, talk about this, that there is a story to be told, a dream to be had. An immersion in an insoluble process, a telling, a tall tale, a told tale, stories that can't be heard, won't be told or talked of & then, like that, the story evaporates by the end of every paragraph, certainly every day.

=-=

LITTLE EXCURSIONS IN THE LAND OF BURNING BRIDGES

We have entered the Age of Incommensurability — as I tag it. The present is all that matters and the past can be swept away. The past is another planet. Figures from the past can only appear to us as contemporaries with a mindset like our own.
—Lindsay Waters (The Enemy of Promise)

We are just beginning to write the first sentences of other stories…
—Christa Wolf

The evening runs on like this until then. Or there. Pillars of smoke scattered along the horizons, columns of refugees traversing the countryside. Try to imagine this. Which to lash to the roof of the car, the mattress or the winter tires? But will you remember winter tires if this story is taking place in July? Meanwhile, a pair of robins duel on the lawn as a blackbird puffs itself out in ardor. Or there…

Where is another path, another road? All indicators suggest incipient failure as roadside trash accumulates in the passage. Someone who remembers peacetime is up ahead honking their horn at the hesitation in movement. Here a pile of trash, there remnants of a meal. Newspapers, discarded furniture, a row of sweaters and shoes, the hulk of a broken down Honda pushed into the ditch. Beyond the tree line, the stench of exhaust fumes, the rumble of another caravan running towards this same eventual disappointment on another blocked avenue of escape. Like formations of geese crisscrossing an early winter twilight.

A weekend of slowing and shorter tracking shots as these columns of refugees clot into communities, a highway of shantytowns. Remember Godard's Weekend? Cortazar's The Southern Thruway? Those caravan encampments set up at the rest areas on the A1 when we visited Ireland in 1985? Circuits of travel growing smaller and smaller even as we move away from the smoke, the fires, the journey finally downgraded to day trip, our exodus a renewed exploration of here as soccer moms find themselves delegated supply sergeants, parsing out Luna bars and bottle of Dajani as emergency rations to school buses filled with other parent's children.

Later, in the city, there is a proliferation of interest in the writing of Christa Wolf as writing workshops readdress autobiography and creative non-fiction, a response by area instructors to the strangeness of this new now. "File them," they say, "file them and leave it alone for now. This now. Or tomorrow. Or better yet the next day, or the day after that." And then, for now, be content in a telling moment. A simple movement. Tonight's assignment: explore being unalone. Be inspired in the realization that we thought salvation would be individual. But rather, it is social, like survival. This is the lure of the rapture. And the lie.

=-=

"Robin Hood was right" on the bumper of an SUV

-=-

the audacity of survival
to simply be here

=-=

Echoes. There's something else going on here. Something in-definite. The conversation is punctuated by the long silences that come with comfort. A clutter of smiles on the shelf rear-ranged as the song goes on. Something stretched, rubbed the wrong way. What was the name of that band? All of yester-day's parties played and replayed. Punch in a room. The fan slowly turns. A hand reaching into a pocket. Before the long damp smell of low tide, the steady attack of high tide against the restraining wall. Hapless Bastards. The elongated stretch of sand. A do it yourself project. Console or console? Oh all right, call it a beach. Confusing the shortness of time with a shortness of breath. A buoy marker driven towards the shore ahead of a storm. Someplace else the waters all may taste of plastic. A desperate form of healing. The fingers come out of the pockets with a bit of sand. Strands of seaweed swirl in the deeper pools. A heartbeat is mimicked. Select a smallish rectangle of plywood from the scrap pile. The lazy scrawl of a snail in the wet sand. Select a handful of nails of various sizes. He is fascinated by the television where a man is talking, justifying illegal actions as he explains the nature of a greater good, a higher cause. Drive the nails into the wood. Drive on deeper into the woods. Birds in flight. Now pluck the nails, or bow them. How do we make our silences as interesting as our sounds? Change the terminology. Explore the circular motion of wire against metal. This is music and this is sound. Fingers again touch a bit of sand at the bottom of a pocket. A silence that is total and real is of course impossible. Challenge the terminology. The needle comes down with a pok and the room fills with static. Can a candy wrapper and a book lying on a desktop a year from now trigger the same response that a Reese's Peanut Butter Cup and Philip Whalen's On Bear's Head triggers now as you look up from the tableau into the afternoon? "End fact, try fiction" pounded into you. There's no turning back. A clutter of smiles on the shelf. The world is full of rooms where a phone sits ringing. Kate's fingerprints on the window before the afternoon light can assert itself. A collection of homemade musical instruments and back in town the fan slowly turns. The boy is fascinated by the television. Birds in flight. He'd tried to think of soft words, of

soft sounds, the surfaces of snow, of stars, the motions within bodies of water. A finger traces sand along the seam of
a pocket. Informed words in the circular motion of winds.
What happened to the song that we knew so well? Walking
a row of cars to get a view of one of the last manned light
houses on the southern coast of Maine. A cumbersome sentence for such a beautiful night. The sea crashing across the
rocks, phosphorescence. Jump along the rocks. In the morning the tide is out and it's just another postcard, and anyway,
it's gone the way of automation now. Think of found sounds,
unfound sounds, the informed words of concatenation. But
now he's not sure that is what he wanted to say. Rub grains
of sand between thumb and forefinger. Another Sunday. All
that could remain are the sounds of peace, of love. Cider jelly
and croissants. The words that we reach for are the words
we might choke on. Take a length of wire between the fingers
and rub gently the nails. He's wanted to make some kind of
start. The way that a slow melody from a saxophone can remind you of Veronica. The hand in a pocket laced with sand.
Read the paper. Coffee steaming, sunlight streaming into the
room. He writes: he is writing that he is sitting across the
room. The still, heavy air of August. He writes: Let the cup of
coffee cool. "My peace I give…" the wonder of the nameless
things. The cats sit in a window and watch a rabbit sitting in
the backyard. He writes: a glass of ice tea by a dish of ripe
plums. The grass is wet and long and a dark, dark green. Art,
Messianism and crime. "My peace I leave you." Something
else about composition. He writes: He holds within himself

so much innocence, and I wonder where is the justice as I look at a picture of Wesley as a baby leaning against the television exploring the features of Oliver North with his tiny hand. Sip coffee and wonder if this doesn't happen every morning. The world is filled with sounds you will never recognize, never comprehend. Smear a finger through a dollop of dripped jelly. Gather up the last crumbs, bring your dish and cup to the kitchen. This is music and this is sound. Turn off the coffee. He thinks about a score and drags a nail across a piece of wood and it becomes a rhythmic thing against the grain and he thinks again about a score. The fan slowly turns. A hand in a pocket comes away with beach sand from last summer. This is sound and this is music. Let the words through you but never over you. The tide is coming in.

=-=

WIR FAHREN NOCH EINMAL NACH AMERIKA
There will be something like the idea of roads, of highways, a landscape, an endless procession of small towns, don't litter placards and what used to be called roadside eateries. Not these things you see, not the drive-ins, not the desperate housewives running away in oversized station wagons, not the smokestacks of factories belching clouds of who knows what into the evening light, not the farmlands, the verdant fields, the indescribable splendor of the woodlands of the hinterland and certainly not the hinterland, none of these things, just the idea of them. Sitting in the living room, or at a kitchen table, or draped across the bed or leaning over

a lunch counter. "We're coming to America again," he said back there at the beginning. The memory, the image, the idea of conjuring travelers, Jack and Neal going cross-country, or Peter and Dennis, or Thelma and Louis or Phil and Sal or Jack and Jill going cross-country on a movie screen say, and William Burroughs sitting in an auditorium watching A Knife in the Head, or Karl May wherever he might be sitting and watching a Knife in the Head, or better yet, Big Bill and Karl sitting together down at the Nickelodeon watching a Knife in the Head and smiling at each other after Bruno Ganz says, "An American in my situation would just start shooting out the window," and then Karl May and William Burroughs would go home and reinvent Montana, and having it their way, as Burger King might say.

-=-

Out there in the nowhere.

=-=

"So this is how it goes. Last night I had a dream about a dream I had the night before. The dream itself is incredibly mundane. It's happening while I'm watching a movie on the late show, back when there used to a show called the late show. It's a shoot'em up. A Walking Tall kind of movie (Buford Pusser? Remember Joe Don Baker? The Rock remade it a little while back, which gives you an idea of when I'm writing this version.) Anyway, the movie's called "Season of

Terror," and the dream part of the dream was living through the movie as you watch it. On the screen there's a knock on the door and I watch myself get up to answer it. And in the next instant I am answering it, which in itself isn't too bad. The other dreamy part is that I didn't remember that I'd had this dream the night before until last night when I dreamt about watching part 2 of the movie, and knowing what would happen next when I was watching the movie. I knew I didn't want to get involved in the movie again. I told everyone in the house not to answer the door, ignore the telephone. But the first time there was a knock at the door, the same thing happened again. There I was getting up to open the door, walking across the room, opening the door and I was back in the movie again, and even though I don't usually remember my dreams, I knew these guys were after me and I didn't know who they were. And I didn't know who to talk to about this, so I've written it down here for you. I hope you don't mind ..." He read the entry over and over, trying to remember when he wrote it. But it never seems to get past being silly. As he tried to forget it and the dream and get back to the poem he was working on, there was a knock at the door.

-=-

"So I was thinking…we could put together a punk rock band. Call it Les Miserable & the Revolution, or maybe the Sans Culottes … or maybe THE culottes. And we'd only do punk rock covers of songs from Les Miz. I smell big bucks at PBS pledge times. Whatya think?" "You smell big bucks. I smell law suits."

=-=

I'd rather laugh than cry but increasingly the choice is no longer mine. The world flies away or the world pulls away or the
world is pulled away. I stare at the page, ponder it. "It was
as if our lives were a solar system." I can't help but marvel at
the self-referential, if that's the phrase I'm looking for. As if
our lives were a solar system. I really did compare Linda and
myself to binary stars one time, binary stars held together in
a steady pirouette across the cosmos. It was a bad poem or
a paragraph I never showed her or anyone else. Until now.
And now we're just something on the surface of a something
at the mercy of a gravity or what have you. Is there anything
to the downturn in my focus? Do I need a response? Do I
shrug a shoulder? Do marigolds get planted? Do weeds get
pulled? Clean out the cellar, the gutters, the bookcases, thin
out the closets? Maybe it's enough to introduce tofu into the
diet, and you eat it for the same reasons our parents got stuck
with atomic energy: because someone told you it was for
your own good and a money-saver to boot. Never mind, just
make sure that you add two new words to your vocabulary
every week. This week's words: vengeance and refusal. But
you can still hide your meaning in words, especially someone
else's words. "There must be some kind of way out here,"
for example. You can take up the habit of saying things like,
"I haven't been ironic for years," and of course you have to
say it ironically. You can come up with new projects like rereading the Tao Te Ching, or Gertrude Stein, or Proust, and

maybe try to apply this edge of active criticism to the way you look at the world. You've been thinking about critical analysis as if thinking about critical analysis were the same as walking along the edge of the proverbial cliff (as opposed to, say, walking along the edge of the Grand Canyon), trying to watch your step and the view at the same time. But instead you keep thinking about the sun as so many millions, no billions, BILLIONS of tons of tofu, tofu that spits huge flares of, like seitan out from its surface and sends bursts of energy into the ionosphere, energy transformed into the Aurora Borealis, brilliantly illumined waves of color generated by the energy of spectacular displays of fluctuating bean curd. The imagination overpowers irony, and suddenly there is no room for irony in your life, or for even the vaguest suggestion of the critique. Time, as they say, is short and the stakes are way, way too high. Transition is a luxury we can no longer afford, you think, standing by the ocean, speculating that old waves and new waves don't exist. In the end there is only the water. When anything goes, or maybe when everything goes, what are we to be left with? Peter Fuller has written, "those who relinquish the imaginative component in expression inevitably end up reducing art to the state of ideology (or advertising)." Goethe and Schiller much earlier griped, "one can read entire books that have beautiful style and contain nothing at all." I often find myself caught up between these two not so different poles when I look at my work, and finding myself in this zone of intent I will often give myself over to silence, a silence that is almost ideological. To keep quiet not because I don't have anything to say, but to keep quiet because

I don't know how to say what I believe I have to say. But if I believe that language can bring us together why should I let art tear us apart? Stop giving experts their due. Trucks are passing through unsuspecting urban populations loaded with exhausted tofu rods, heading for the large dumping grounds in North Carolina where the nation's spent alternative protein wastes are stored. I say something and it turns up in your work, you say something and it ends up in mine. A new satin letter jacket or a new haircut. Personal hygiene raised to the level of personal statement. I sometimes wonder if I don't write a poem or pick up the guitar for the same reason I use toothpaste or change my underwear. Is a new hairdo the same as a new painting? Is chopping off an arm the same as trimming a tree? If Andre Breton had been a Libyan diplomat, London might be a ghost town. "Pizza beer hot dogs, pizza beer hot dogs", the crowd at the ball park chants late one night at an out of control game. "You're boring, you're boring, you're boring", is the next cheer they yell at the home team. The question is finally how long before I become what I declaim? Of course that question was very ironic. Imagine that. Increasingly it seems that the only thing irony can guarantee is funding. The guarantee that you can only be as neutral as you think your technology is. And yet to say turning back is another way of turning away is not the same as saying turning away is another way of turning back. To write down the note. To stare at it. It was as if their lives were a solar system. I'd rather laugh than cry but increasingly the choice is no longer mine.

=-=

PORTENDS

When you're losing your grip, everything seems important. A glance your way, that blinking light, the sound of a car horn, all gain significance.

-=-

ESCAPE VELOCITY

an unsolicited remix of Alvin Lucier's I Am Sitting In A Room

i am sitting in a room different from the one you are sitting in. it is filling with thoughts of escape velocity, of a velocity that is attained by a moving object (as a rocket) that would enable it to escape from the gravitation field of the earth (or a celestial body) and move outward in space. i am recording the sound of my speaking voice in relation to this room. the chairs, the drapes, that ceramic cockatoo, that Max Ernst print, even the quartz heater that just snapped on and these binoculars by my notebook are joining in the recording of this story. To be played into the room again and again to hopefully achieve the title of this remix. words degenerating into letters, into characters moving alone together in a room becoming, in a sense, the room, articulated by speech, a speech hopefully anonymous, the sources of this story eventually joining the characters of this story as they break up and away, speeding off into a new existence where any semblance

of this story, with perhaps the exception of its rhythms, will
be destroyed.

-=-

"...the twisted inside of a human heart for instance..."
—radio voice 9/16/02

*

"...after i came, which is the extent of my recollection"
—Donald Rumsfeld, DOD press conference 9/16/02

=-=

BASED ON TRUE EVENTS
—a historical novel in a few sentences

They lie to us. There was change in the air. Born, not asked, and the world is perched on the verge of was. Of course the only solution can be another choice. Has-beens and wannabes queue everywhere to offer their versions of salvation while planners meet and make recommendations. Once the choice is made and nothing changes it is clear that blame will be left to us or the way things are, and so it goes, the fade from is to was, from where to war. That inevitable, that simple.

-=-

ON NOT HAVING THE BALLS OF ANI DI FRANCO
so one day i'm at work and find myself critiquing the way people were using language in a meeting i'd just attended. They were talking about family slotted classification systems, career tracking, the myriad pools and channels of money that kept passing us by in the organization, and suddenly i hear myself describing myself as a former writer. It made a certain amount of sense saying this as I hadn't really been writing that much in the last couple of years. When asked, i had any number of reasons to account for the stoppage, but that afternoon it felt my inactivity indicated it was time to acknowledge there was something more than writer's block at work here. Maybe after 2 years the Muse had given up on me and

stopped visiting, and i spent the rest of the afternoon thinking that was almost worth writing down and then of course didn't as, and this you already know, i was deep in a period of writer's block. The next morning, during a phone conversation in which an extended metaphor was offered to me, the previous day's metaphor was recalled and in the recounting the metaphor grew and mutated and the Muse became the woman who drops off the meals on wheels lunch at the door of my trailer. As the days pass, she notices that those chicken pot pies she's been leaving me are starting to pile up on the stoop until one lunchtime the Muse finally says, "Fuck him," and crosses my name off that big, big list of hers, and she gets back into that big old van of hers and moves on deeper into the trailer park, not noticing me as i come barreling out the door of my trailer and start running after her, waving a piece of paper with these few lines written on it, which never even mention what this has to do with the title "on not having the balls of ani di franco."

-=-

FROM A Kind of Motion called Heat

Part 6. Why hesitate? Thought about not talking about it, then thought better, like thinking about talking honestly in a second language when you can hardly do it in your first one. Maybe there's nothing here for us. This might be more like an exercise rather than what we might call a sustained work of imagination. Maybe I should have said something else, something a little more reassuring. You've heard this someplace else, or seen it, done it, read it, said it. Another voice, another time. I should try to keep this fresh if nothing else. Something that might keep you in your chair, or turning the page. A certain kind of restraint the way I might use my mind to bend forklifts. One contemplates paroxysm of guilt and reaches for the dictionary. The wonder of the raconteur raised to poetry as we contemplate a new world. If only we didn't have to survive after a certain fashion. The lure of the café, the public life. But one must always know when to stop. Lower the head, lean into the table. Remember this guy? The other writing, or waiting in anticipation for the answer, the retort. Now we finally resort to an inadequate vocabulary. The powerless response to the demonstration of power. An articulated desire. Something off the TV: "I'm a trusting guy. Spell that j-e-r-k.". Cue the audience. Home again. Umbrellas folded, chairs stacked, used paper cups all thrown away. Coming back or going on, with the chance for crossing paths. Nothing signifies loss like loss. Remember "Be realistic, Demand the impossible!" Someplace between dream and version a car noses into the street. There is a growing familiarity here in this night as you become aware of what is beyond the darkness, as this awakening is making this more than a dream and recalled features are transformed, rendered applicable to the developing interdiction. A kind of motion we call heat. Maybe overgrowth has overwhelmed another memory and created nostalgia. As you write this, you listen to a duo of Chinese zither and violin over the sigh of night traffic, the softish throb of a police car's siren into the scene as these words spool out into the mise en scène.

=-=

There is a sound like filigree, or filament, repartee, or effervescence – say sunset. Simultaneity: my vocabulary is letting go. Rainfall tables, or on the table a meal of stew and powder biscuits. A basket of hot powder biscuits and a big pot of steaming stew. Mmmm. Through an open window a tree shaking itself bare rustles loudly, and against the screen, a branch scratches. An effervescence. The "roil' of a wave, or rolling waves, slowed by the cold. The ocean returns, and I'm sitting at a table in a cottage, before a plate of croissants and a jar of apple butter. A pattern of crumbs scattered down my shirt. Naw, it's really my living room, and it's a snack of English muffins and apricot preserves. The ballgame is on with the sound off. I love the way the fans yell and nothing comes out, Steve Garvey rolling across that plastic infield silently, the way in a movie a pickup truck sails over the crest of a hill out into the deadened space. And beyond the window behind me, the sun comes and goes, the leaves running from yellow and brown to gold and back with it, and it's fall again. I turn off the ballgame, and turn the page. I can't remember where Linda is on this lost day. I can't remember where anyone is but there's a sound like filigree, or filament, as delicate as it sounds as it signals: somebody knows how long Edison searched for the material to use as the filament in his electric bulb. I read about it once. At times I can feel a certain repartee with all the world. Other times, nothing at all. There is an effervescence to the end of daylight. Sunset, say, or twilight.

i just checked Rosmarie's Waldrop book on Edmond Jabes, Lavish Absences, out of the library. This fact, this event, lends itself to a brief discussion here of this break, the block, this leave from my writerly duties that these fragments not only represent, but are pulling me out of. Maybe it wasn't a block at all. Maybe we can think of it as a vacation from my vocation. Last summer i tried to get myself back to work by sitting at this very machine typing out pages from my notebook. The passages came to several pages that i felt compelled to read at Dave and Sharon's backyard reading a week later. Afterwards, Dave took me aside to tell he hoped his next block was so productive. Why did i stop writing? Too often, too quickly, i blame my father, his death, thinking that maybe a hesitation in my life coincided with the conclusion of his, and that there's a sense that what i should write about is him. But how? Or should that be why? More guiltily i fear that it may not be him i want to write about but rather my sense of his ending. In other words, i just want to write about me some more, and we all know there's enough of that. Is it time to write? Is there time to write? In the Museum of Unconditional Surrender, Dubravka Ugresic writes, "the album and autobiography are by their very nature amateur activities, doomed from the outset to failure and second-rate ness. That is, the very act of arranging pictures in an album is dictated by our unconscious desire to show life in all its variety, and as a consequence life is reduced to a series of dead fragments.

Autobiography has similar problems in the technology of remembering; it is concerned with what once was, and the trouble is that what once was is being recorded by some who is now." So where does Pop fall into this? Or me, or even those months leading up to the month of the Poet's Mimeo show? Is it the past or the project? Fear to remember, or fear to relate? Beats me.

=-=

And who will we listen to tonight, love struck or dumbstruck, starting out again on this path across the white wilderness of the page into another period of war daze. Who can tell? Which is it, traitors in waiting, or demand? Watching the clouds gather what else is there to do but find a name for the soundtrack. Armageddon Dub? Apocalypso?

-=-

Steps across the border
"To overcome the centralized message," those sanctioned un-questioning voices posing as new and art. The noise of the dream — le bruit de la reve — dancing to keep time, to kill time, to be alive. In a documentary, after Fred Frith ruminates on society and his role as provocateur against the normal flow of information to individuals through performing and trying to make people aware of the world around them, comes one of the better endings for a film i've seen in a while — an elderly couple dancing on a platform while waiting for a train — who

knows what they are dancing to — his or her humming, mu-
zak, the drone of the station master on the intercom — but
the sound in the film is one of Frith's lovely little songs and
the effect is beautiful, the couple hopping tiny steps in the cold
morning, their breath dancing around them like clouds as the
train slowly pulls in. Lovely.

=-=

JLG Lift, or

EXPLICIT ESTIMATION OF BOTH MUTATION AND
SELECTION BIAS FOR THE PURPOSE OF UNDER-
STANDING PROSE FUNCTION AND EVOLUTION: AP-
PLICATION TO HUMAN ENDURANCE

It ended, as in the manner of most human relations, badly.
Another night a stride behind as beyond, on the horizon, the
appearance of another dawn beckoned once more. Put down
the pen. Pick up the page. Then consider Merz, or perhaps
the state of collage in the Golden Age. 12 minutes gone, and
a sense that something has to go next is manifest. Look at
a book of collages by John Evans and marvel at the lack of
political correctness that accumulated in the detritus of the
pre-Globalization era, as well as in the creation of an art for
one's personal collection. Consider Aunt Jemina selling Indian cigarettes or "Monkeys Violate the Heaven Palace" fire-
works as you marvel at the handiwork of the artist. Call it
displacement, better yet a revelatory indifference considered

as a plausible, even viable, endpoint. Apologies can only accumulate as the misunderstandings continue.

Looking back, I did less than nothing. I wrote, and then I didn't write; or wouldn't write. And then, to only return to writing by writing that the fact of fiction is tiring. Why else do we pick up a novel or a book of short stories before we go to sleep? Decant the situation while listening to the answering machine and flipping through the day's mail. Perhaps we find our reading leading us to a lack of uniqueness. The sun going down, say, or the hill going a wavy green when viewed through the glass of those hundred year old window panes. Timeshare effluvia leading us on to binding aggravations like the possibility that fiction is written to be tiring, if not tiresome. A wordless response emailed into the void to fill the void. Better yet, call it a cry, a plea for understanding.

Someplace in the house, a glass broke. He turned to me. "Please don't call me stranger." "Stranger than what?" I want to ask, but the moment passes. Was it indifference or something less significant as we listened as the silence ascended? What's going on here, you want to ask, a function of imagination or a manifestation of memory? Cindy Sherman or Hannah Schygula, he thinks, as if once again daring to turn off the subtitles while watching a Tarkovsky movie. We'll simply pretend that all of the comings and goings in the courtyard are natural, perhaps even real.

The fictive projection isn't taking hold, is it? It's just you and me, this room and these words passing between us. An objective is looming there in the landscape, an aleatoric indicator as the sunlight streams across it, even as my word checker tells me something is wrong. Aleatoric is not in its vocabulary. My word checker suggests alternatives. Electric, it lists, aleuronic, or lavatory. Then Plethoric, followed by electronic, allotropic, and finally clitoris. A curious digression that somehow lends itself to the very word in question. A tonic to the sad story of sentences that find themselves in the service of only a plot. No description please, we're narrating. Aleatoric isn't in my vocabulary either, just my practice. We're also running late, and a gull cuts across the morning, gray and cold in early May. The aesthetics of the destitute, and here's Joni singing River and I wish I could say it was over but it's not for me to say. The specter of underage drinking haunts the landscape as ex-lushes scramble for higher ground. The connection is so slow this morning even as we live in a beautiful world where the coffee is strong and the breezes are warm. There's an elasticity to the moment as someone notes somewhere that the strippers are only just now going to sleep and somewhere else someone is playing his guitar, and he lays into the distortion pedal, and a heady fuzz permeates the moment, while someplace else someone is brought from sleep by the sound of a key entering a lock at the other end of the house.

Which is the conceit: that from time to time I might take advantage of my role as storyteller and interrupt my story with an embellishment or a commentary? Or my telling you that from time to time I might take advantage of my role as storyteller and interrupt my story with an embellishment or a commentary? Even now, back here in the midst of all this normality, uncertainty is still uncovered, as every night long lines of traffic exit the city like a kind of Whitmanesque colloquialism, and even though no agents of the police or any other security agency have ever arrested me or a member of my family, I go to sleep confident in my belief that we are living on the verge of a fascist state. Yet there are still the infinitesimal vistas. The remembered click in the sound of the turned knob, and the eventual glow of the dial pushed out of the radio like dawn ahead of the rising sun. The room filling with the ebb and flow of washes of static as you slowly turned the dial past newscasts, farms reports, ball scores, distant talk shows, lonely dj monologues, stopping only at a song, and resting there only long enough to be unsatisfied. And now the pain as the pen slides to a stop at another elaboration of this moment. We listen to the phone ring impassively, the ambiguity of the modifier –adverb? adjective? – now lost as the phone remains unanswered, an unopened conduit to the outside world. Searching for a response even as the ringing cuts off – no message left – askew in the confidence of unfounded speculations, and the phone is ringing again.

As you may recall, tomorrow will be wonderful. Standing in a window, someone will watch the day unfold recalling the first time she heard Jimi play the introduction to Voodoo

Child (Slight Return). Lose your clean eye with delusion and vexation, a Lotus prayer begins at the start of Lotus of the True Law. A where no longer there, a song of distant shores, an honest trade. "We work for nothing," she says, sitting with her husband at the kitchen table. A turning away as stylized as that line twixt ocean and us, becoming an elegiac motion towards home. An accumulation of dilemma all over the world might be discovered in these words. Picking up the watch you mutter, "Another night a stride behind as beyond, on the horizon," and to make it fit the line is crossed out. You begin again. It will end, as in the manner of most human relations, badly.

-=-

The city is full of tired flags. Tattered by the wind, in the traversal of the city, ragged as they splay from car antennas, or faded and torn, taped on doors and windows. Everywhere patriotism trumps proper flag etiquette as ADD, maybe, mixes with xenophobia in some neglectful variation on patriotism.

-=-

a sad realization. Don Van Vliet said it happened to him on his way to kindergarten when at a street corner he pulled his mother back onto the curb and out of the path of a car. He realized right then that those in charge were just as clueless in relation to the real world as he was. I can't recall when it first occurred to me. Maybe when I started shoplifting, maybe for

sure when i started shoplifting and just left the stuff I'd taken
on the hoods of parked cars as soon as i left stores, and ended
up just shy of a kind of satori when I started shoplifting from
one store and leaving the stuff i was shoplifting in the store
next door. Anyway, i thought of that Captain Beefheart story
that i first read in Rolling Stone back in 1970 when I found
the following scribbled on an envelope the other day – "...and
now a realization that Western civilization, that Western culture (okay, it's not particularly civilized OR cultured so let's
just call it Western Reality), that Western reality is probably
based on scads and scads of misreadings of bad translations
of pirated anonymous texts. and how's that for clueless?"

-=-

We began the day early – note the curious blend of appro-
priation and dominion already apparent even as the day had
clearly started much earlier of its own accord, unbeknownst
to my decision to include you all in this vignette. We sat on
the porch, the morning sun warm and warming on our necks,
gathering ourselves as we sipped from a glass of grapefruit
juice. Days later back home in Vermont we will read on a vid-
eocassette container the slogan "enterrons les morts et non la
verité," on a young Rwandan's t-shirt, but for now in southern California the plan is much less formidable and somber.
Perhaps a few words strung together in a notebook, some
humor, a snapshot now and again as we look up from our
reading. A sudden wet clatter as two birds take advantage
of the standing water in the fountain in the front yard. We

look from the birds to a pile of postcards sitting on a small table, a few short hellos waiting to radiate out from this deck on a house on a street in a neighborhood in Orange County to destinations scattered across the homeland, messages that might have been just that much more interesting if we'd started writing them now instead of earlier in the less defined moments of the morning. Regardless, it's the day after Super Tuesday and two birds taking advantage of the standing water in the fountain in the front yard have been barely noticed until now. All we can be sure of is a lot of comings and goings back and forth inside in the kitchen as the family stirs, and the occasional sounds of passing traffic in the street beyond the front yard. Infinite shuffle as the MP3 player recommends. There is the bright new green of grass edging the blackened remains of trees and shrubs across the hills surrounding the house. There is the steady rhythm of a tethered orange balloon rising and falling above the Orange County Great Park. Much closer, there is a mockingbird picking at a pile of macadamia nuts on the table on the other end of the porch as we whisper, "Try writing that at home." In the house we can hear the candidates' trade accusations in film clips on the morning news with no hint at the ongoing discussion taking place elsewhere in the room on the comparative sociology of advanced marginality. There is a promise of a Cobb salad at Citrus City Grille, a Nissan Infiniti passing us on the Freeway, a 12" single of a remix of Pat Benetar's Love is a Battlefield waiting to be found in an Orange City antique shop, a particularly tasty Marguerita waiting to be assembled later that afternoon in a hotel bar and enjoyed as we sit on a deck looking out over the Pacific in Laguna beach. But in the meantime, it is still early morning on a holiday Wednesday where we read, where we sip grapefruit juice, where we contemplate without even knowing it a new kind of poverty on both sides of the Atlantic, a poverty in which we may perhaps eventually become one with our brothers and sisters in the underdeveloped regions of the world. There are villages in the deserts, villages in the forests, villages by the rivers; there is a village down the road but its citizens call their village a town, and a stranger is riding into town with a new set of promises. Mr. Carson at the general store sees a new creditor, while Amy at the saloon spots a new John, and Mr. Greevy the undertaker looks for a gun and holster and the possibility of more business, and, finally, Jenny, that young woman crossing the street, wonders if this one might be the drifter that frees her from this one-horse town. Unfortunately, the rider, sitting comfortably in the back seat of the town's only cab, is merely a consultant hired by the library at the nearby medical school. Amongst his charges: perform a "Customer Service" Workshop, with follow-up in-house one-on-one training for key personnel; based on results of the workshop, proposals for future follow-up training expressed in a planning document, to review recent reference desk installation re: staffing issues, collection resources to support reference service, and review IT equipment inventory for planned ICT Classroom in a completed Excel document, suitable for submission to a granting organization. Much later back home in Vermont we will read Marcel Pagnol's description of laugh-

ter as a "song of triumph. It expresses the laugher's sudden discovery of his momentary superiority over the person at whom
he is laughing. That explains bursts of laughter in all times in
all countries." But here, the glass, once filled with grapefruit
juice, is finally empty, and, having avoided its being utilized in
some obvious clichéd humorous observation, sits on the table.
A shutter snaps and the morning is caught forever, even as a
story is still unfolding.

=-=

Specious or speechless; the goal of unlearning or the goad of
unlearning?

-=-

Caught Again

As if it only happens in the rain. This idea of descent. Jan
and I could be walking across a field. It could be sunset. Or
early morning. But it is afternoon. And not raining. We are
sitting at a table. There is music, a waitress, men sitting at the
bar. Or not. Jan nonchalants it. A hand through his hair as
he says, "Maybe they don't even matter." Steam rising from
a coffee cup. They're all coming back. "Don't forget heartache," Jan says, wagging a finger at me. "Wilhelm Reich said
that heartache was the proof of human emotions. A hollow
ache or an hollow ache in the upper chest." I laughed. "Or the
hollow ache." Jan laughed in agreement, even as he watched
someone cross the room. Then down, to stare into his water

glass. But save that. A funny story, not like this one. Let's go back to that walk in the field. Or on the beach. A picnic. A bonfire. There's Josh, staggering into the water, then diving in, swimming after the sun. Of course you had to be there. Ah yes, caught again. Sitting on the rocks, the hills behind us going to blue, to gray. Later, we walked arm in arm back to and past the fire, heading back to the city, to homes, to each other. Ah heartache, heartache. All I ever seem to get is heartache. But really... "The clown's philosophy is based on the assumption that everyone is a fool; and the greatest fool is he who doesn't know he is a fool." Looking up from the driver's seat, Jan grins at me, knowing where this loose rambling is heading. His grin edges towards a leer and then he's gone, his car kicking up dust and rattling pebbles as it crosses the parking lot. Between the rock and ... anyway, that's the way it goes, short little escapades with no beginning, no end. Just glimpses. The sense of descent is in the fall. The secret is you don't have to reign and it doesn't have to rain.

=-=

TV on, sound off. listening to records one last time before selling them. This one's a weak late period Monk — so long Thelonious and another farewell to the label of completist — and across the bottom of the screen at Headlines News, a headline — "Recycle, reuse, German publisher to release novels and poems on toilet paper..." Editorial comment or economic position?

-=-

Maybe the trick is to look for stories the way we look for rain
— out the window, in puddles, signs of movement, contact.
Is that how we do it, how they do it, the poets, the novelists,
the dramatists? Find these stories that hold us trapped, the
characters we will listen to for hours. A torrent of situations,
cascading into heaps of bottles, boxes, scraps of paper. Or
try this: "There's a distant peaceful murmur from the village:
human voices. You want to call them human. As long as they
don't start singing. Their singing is unlike anything he ever
heard in his vanished life: it's from beyond the human level,
or below it. As if crystals are singing: but not like that, either.
More like ferns unscrolling—something old, carboniferous,
but at the same time newborn, fragrant, verdant." No, that's

not me. It's Margaret Atwood in Oryx & Crake. i've got nothing like that, except for maybe a version of that original sound she's looking to describe. Maybe 20 years ago, a spring evening and we're standing out in the front yard, listening to the rustle of wet leaves settling and thinking we're listening to the sound of seedlings pushing out of the ground. And there was this raccoon watching us from under the bush just wanting to tell us that it didn't sound like singing at all, atall, atall.

=-=

1ST VERSION FOR TERRI SCHIAVO

You want to say that the dream is an elaboration of yesterday, a moment stretched into an afternoon maybe, or three weeks in another country. Suddenly, the trees along the road are all unfamiliar, the bird songs unrecognizable, the rattle of insect wings immense. Meanwhile, the freshly turned fields of open earth unleash the rich stink of spring, while here moulting snow shrinks away to piles of soggy pebbles and unmelted salt. A reflector lies on the median as a leaden disco tune spills from a car out into the afternoon. As you add to this inventory of the day's detritus, in front of the court house they pray, as they prey and pry into her life, and though you want to preserve this afternoon of shoes and parking meters, the harmonies of brakes sounding along the cries of passing baby carriages, or the slide of sunlight and shadow along the wall of the courthouse as the sun pushes aside the clouds and sends the afternoon all glowy into an advancing springtime, you wish you had the courage to roll down the window and scream, "Just let the woman fucking die."

Recipe

There is, he writes, a certain ease like learning to cook, or cleaning the car, or writing down a thought. This thought. It's so easy. The air is so clean, they say, the water so clear. To discern the marketing ploy. Left for a job in the city. Where are the fish? Where are the simple soothing words that can put an end to this? A narrative that can lead us out of here. A door opens. The room is filling with people. They are wearing bandanas obscuring their features. Slice the carrots, the peppers, chop the onions. Crush a clove of garlic, two, three. The noise will start to build. Form a single line. An alarm in the street, an answering siren in the distance. Everyone is going to the cellar with clean sheets. A vacuum cleaner is thrown down the stairs. A bucket of sudsy water. A child is singing, a guitar is being strummed. Storm clouds rush across the sky. Dead fish mottle the lake. Trash fish appear on dinner plates. Someone is asking how dinner is coming. Dice the potatoes. Overcoats begin to pile on the couch. Brown 3 pounds of stew meat cut into 1 inch cubes. Put on a sweater. Form a line. Have a drink. Use the typewriter. Send the kids outside. It's starting to rain. Sprinkle soap powder on the car. Another sheet of paper. Don't let anyone else in the house, not even the kids. Instead, throw sponges outside through second floor windows. Ignore the sirens. Leave the windows open and let the rain in. Pick up the phone. Call friends and ask them to pour soap powder into the fountains around the city. Call the neighbors and tell them to wear bandanas to obscure their features. When the police arrive, send them next door. Cover the meat with stock or water in the largest pot you can find. Strike up a conversation with a Jehovah's Witness through the locked front door as the kids sneak into the house through a cellar window. Call a radio station and have them announce a surplus cheese and fish giveaway at City Hall. Call another radio station and request martial music. Call the talk radio station call in program and demand martial law. Close the windows. Watch the rain. Lock the cellar door. Combine the remaining ingredients, season, and bring to a boil. Reduce the heat. Simmer.

-=-

LONDON IN RUINS, AS IMAGINED BY GUSTAVE DORE, IN 1873

So the world seizes up in another of those paroxysms that seem to be occurring with greater frequency here in the first decade of the twenty-first century and your first response is to power up the sound system. It's London Calling this morning as this week's hotspots pepper the front page – Fallujah, al-Ramadi, Kut. The Ukrainians are pulling out, the Spanish are looking at exit strategies along with the Bulgarians, and the Koreans have taken to their barracks while our boys go toe to toe and door to body bag with their boys for all the wrong reasons, and you're thinking you won't write about this, you won't talk about this, there's no dream to be had, no story to be made from this. It's just another immersion in another insoluble process, I mean unsolvable process, so you, you've got the TV on, reading the headline ticker scrolling across the bottom of the screen as newscasters and pundits flap their gums like some ventriloquism act on public access, all the while jumping around to that Montgomery Clift song on Side 2 (inspirational rhyme Nembutal, alcohol) trying not to tell a tall tale, a told tale, a story that can't be heard or won't be told aloud and then suddenly recalling Dr. Benway someplace saying … "the patient's a job, just a job," and you grow up and you calm down and it's quarter to 8 on another working day.

=-=

Memory a swirl of anecdotes, the desk a litter of notes, the notebook a flurry of beginnings, and the dream was that much simpler than the recounting of it.

AFTER READING ADAM ZAGAJEWSKI'S WATCHING SHOAH IN A HOTEL ROOM IN AMERICA, CERTAIN IDEAS COME TOGETHER

Here in the academy they recommend a certain silence, a certain distance, not unlike the acquiescent silence of the distance that has fallen nearly everywhere in recent times. The academy in question is situated near an airport large enough to support the metropolitan area that the academy is located in. On occasion C-5a military transports will practice short runway approaches and landings there. We might be sitting on the lawn in front of the library having lunch, or perhaps chatting while on break in the mid-afternoon sun, and one of those huge aircraft might crawl out from the tree line and then in a slow arc slide across the edge of the sky, turbines groaning loud into the afternoon. From my work desk on other days I can also watch some of that arc, the groans much less obvious through the window, and sometimes I wonder if these are the same aircraft that carried the bulldozers halfway around the world to bury alive thousands of "our" enemies in the recent war. And helicopters from all over the region use a nearby landing pad when transferring the sick and injured to the medical facility that is affiliated with the academy. Many times these helicopters will pass very low, and sometime I can look up and see the pilots of these helicopters that are sometimes military copters and I imagine that sometimes the pilots can look down and see me as I'm walking the street or mowing the lawn or sitting out in front of the library and I'll wonder if they flew low like this over the road out of Kuwait to Basra and then like now motion to a person seen on the ground, only gave him (or her) the finger, or maybe a sawing motion across his throat like that old Polish railroad worker in Shoah, instead of that slow wave in greeting. Admonition, warning, farewell, curse, greeting, dispassionate and all at once. Maybe it's best left unmentioned, the war I mean, or consigned to a different vocabulary, a different set of experiences. The shorter lines are the domain of love, or landscape. But money changes everything, the song says, becomes ominous, and coercive as any sunset. The wash of color overwhelms any recommendation. A siren in the distance. Did I mention the medical center? Ambulances throughout the city pass through the academy heading for the medical center's emergency facilities. Hearing an ambulance one day while I'm cataloging a copy of Ramsay Clark's study of American war crimes in the Persian Gulf for the library's collection, I ponder the merits of conjuring the headlights of 3 ambulances illuminating a killing field and sending long shadows across the screams of the dying, the kind of black humor that never is on the news, especially on those days when the boys and girls come home, but it turns up later in the histories, the news that was never news, that no one sees, that we store here in the academy, so that there can be news later. The disgust that hindsight brings, a reminder that it wasn't really a war after all.

-=-

Having nothing to say and wanting to say it, to tell it, to put a character here, say, a teacher, say, a writer, say, a salesman or an information specialist to say nothing in such a way that it becomes something you might want to hear again, or read again, here on this page in the lateness of the day or, there, morning, or now, in the sun as he writes, this character we'll call a writer who writes in a tiny notebook these words, or those words, a brief passage about where time passes, a moment really, and gone, like this sentence where nothing has happened even as something was being said, or read, or written, and you look up …

=-=

I used to have perspective, but now I can get by only on hindsight.

-=-

What about the latest manifestation of the changing patterns of life here in late-capitalist America? It seems that everyone talks about a post-lottery existence. "If I win the Megabucks or Powerball or Quick pix" is the latest mantra. Play responsibly, they'll remind us in a few years. We'll all still work, of course, but it's never enough. That's why there's the filter of the dream. Money, success, recognition. The way out. And it can only be achieved by chance, despite the workshops, the handbooks, the hard work, the seventeen most often select-ed numbers available only for the length of this commercial so act now, operators are standing by. Offer of course void in all protectorates and territories, including the District of Columbia. And Vermont. But still he wonders – where are all the new millionaires? Maybe it goes something like this: an anonymous car pulls up to the house at night, a sexually and racially balanced team dressed in black breaks into the house, taking away the winners and their families. Ransom note are left behind to confuse the local law officials. The families are then exterminated and the winnings returned to lottery coffers. This might account for the rapid growth of pots in state lotteries that stimulates the sales of more tickets. The bodies of the winners are processed and used to fertilize public garden plots, even as their lives are continued in letters and postcards to friends and relatives, letter that are postmarked from "overseas." These lives are manufactured by the immense number of MFA equipped graduates from writing programs across the nation, workers indentured to the government to pay off their student loans. These texts are then painstakingly copied by a cadre of forgers gathered up in a recent sweep of organized crime by the Justice Department. "We are happy here," they write on card after card, running fingers down master lists of the winner's friends and relatives. "We are happy here," these hopeful and envious souls read over and over, "we are happy here and awaiting your arrival."

=-=

To anticipate the moment of desire, the dissimilar reaction of practice to the situation. To be able to think out loud, to cut out the middleman of rumination. An air of improvisation documenting the silences, filling the spaces of intent with the meaningless moments of movement. The sound of traffic or water moving through a pipe, some image of the rest of the world passing by. You can feel the rising anticipation. Fear like an ocean, increasing the dominion of content over form, not only here (hear) on the page or in the ear, but in the heart as well.

-=-

Evenings with Howard Garbo

…I didn't go underground. I just stopped talking to the press. It got to be pretty funny. I was calling myself Greta Hughes or Howard Garbo –John Lennon

Ongoing. As opposed to going on. There is a suspicion. An intent. Indent. Candlelight. We watch the baby lying on a blanket in the middle of the floor. No protection. She lies there among her toys. I can't think of anything to say. I leave her alone.
Quote—"he who never does anything never makes mistakes."

So how about some recalled moment: a group of middle-aged women disembark from a bus and file into a Montreal club advertising FEMMES NU, and do it at 2 o'clock in the afternoon. Matinee or auditions? Do you think Lenin had in mind such a petty choice in bourgeois irony when he had his ghostwriters write on the significance of militant materialism?

The dogs are running in packs. We hear them late at night. It is not warm in the room, but it is nonetheless comfortable. The radio is playing, and above the music we can hear the dogs running. Another choice between archetype and cliché? Either way, they do bring us closer together. Linda says she's glad this is only a story.

An aside: in the midst of the writing, there is merriment. There is. It's inherent in the telling. A laugh. The chin chucked. Or a rock. I'll throw a rock. Now all I need is a window. A pain encloses me. A needle in the arm. The new middle class horror. Or escape. "How does it feel to be one of the beautiful people?" Needles make me sick. Maybe more than the bourgeoisie. But then, I can't really say that anymore, can i? At least, not with a straight face. [full disclosure—my salary in 1981 (approximate time of writing this) was $11,065] : end aside

Or we could talk about McDonald's for breakfast. Coffee. Winners and losers. Eggs. Kids. Hall and Oates serenade working women. Then 50 ways to leave your lover. "If he ever said that to me…" Bad coffee gone green in the florescent light. It can start at 8 in the morning. Fork-split muffins, pasteurized American cheese made especially for us. Leonard Cohen should be singing this, but he wouldn't write about breakfast at McDonald's.

Or another room. Amongst the professionals. The Curious. "Yes, it's going to be a panel with an artist, a sculptor, and a dancer. We're going to be talking about being a working artist. It's at SUNY Buffalo, in the spring." You'll be sitting at a wobbly table, in front of a patched curtain. He'll talk of past masters. Of use instead of ownership. Alphabets. Beware of teachers, he'll say. The experts. Experience, he'll say, is a form of paralysis.

At first I was going to change the name of the band to ex-beat-les, but   then I decided to stick with ex-hostages. That'll be funny a little bit longer.

Howard Garbo is eating supper. With his wife and son. Pizza. They are having pizza for supper. Someplace a ra-dio is playing. And someplace else. And someplace else. There are radios on. Radios are playing into rooms. How-ard Garbo is singing everywhere. But not here. Howard Garbo is eating supper with his wife and son. They are eating pizza. Howard Garbo is smiling, smacking his lips. Good pizza. God, I wish I'd had a tape recorder. Ongoing, as opposed to going on.

=-=

At the start of the fifth day of rain, he gave up on the future. The next morning the sun broke through, but he didn't.

-=-

Towards an unfair appraisal of the poetics of
classroom poetry.

The trick is to keep the language at arm's length and let the story
out. If all else fails, paraphrase the poems of Browning or the essays of Auden, and always give in to the lure of the critical pose
and ubiquitous review. Celebrate the indefinite pronoun in case
you think the poem is about you or me, as amongst all of these
narratives in a galaxy of familiar rooms, the poem gives way to
the poet and the words win out over the line. There is a promise
in every slight, and a premise in every sight. A signal of preclu-
sion in the various and variegated greens of spring, evolving beyond the typos and mispronunciations, as enlightened is certainly beyond, or in spite of, correctness; the amorphous grays of a
rainy sky giving way to the paso doble. The treble strings tell her
story. The bass strings thrum above the refrigerator's hum, and
the orange light of the bar surrounds the dancers.

=-=

Wise men say…the old saw. The first refuge. Tools. Or uten-
sils. Or ten sails bunched on the lake. An illustration of a
means of propulsion. Point A to Point B. As suddenly women
are reading the way. Or why. As if only fools rush in. Wise
men stay away but never learn. The pain. The reign of the
male knife. The life undone. The sun. There. On the water.
The heat pushed along ahead of the breeze. Outside and here

or heard. The baby cries. Behind me someone says, " I entrusted my future and wealth to a strong woman." Does he know I'm writing this? And does he know I won't turn to say. "Sometimes, that's the only way we can learn."

=-=

Canada Ponders Space Purchase

What will the Canadians do with it all? Fill it with iced tea? Sprinkler heads? Copper colored 1965 two-door Plymouth Satellites? Busloads of junior high school musicians? Tarmacs the size of the Northern Territories? "As Long as He Needs Me." Out of nowhere. May 22 the world will end. Patty Duke reruns. Episode 614: a young girl makes friends with congenial British rock stars Peter and Gordon. Guest stars: Jan and Dean with really broad cockney accents. No, it would have been Chad and Jeremy. Real Britons if not real rock stars. And about Patty Duke —She's now Patty Duke Astin. She's all grown up, and waiting for the end of the world with the rest of us. Remote control garage doors. Decaying fallout shelters. The viscous attempt at dawn, color smeared across the mountains, the horizon. Patty Duke Astin is drinking Carnation Instant Breakfast on the veranda. The news is on. Good Morning America. Inflation. Hostages. No gas. Fucking Arabs (but not out loud), fucking Cubans (but not out loud), fucking Russians (but not out loud). The Pope says to cool it. A jet flies low over the veranda. Patty Duke Astin recognizes it to be a Russian MIG 23 and doesn't know how, even as Patty Duke Astin imagines herself as Paula Prentiss in that scene where she's a plane spotter in 1942 in Otto Preminger's In Harm's Way, and John Wayne comes up to her remote look-out post on a Hawaiian hill to tell that her husband Tom Tryon is missing in action, and Paula Prentiss stares at John Wayne and gulping back tears, swings her binoculars up over his shoulder to look at an airplane passing overhead and Paula Prentiss speaks into her mouthpiece to tell someone off-camera that she's spotted a B-17 or a PBY passing over her look-out post on a hill in Hawaii, and Patty Duke Astin has another thought and runs through the open French door off the veranda and across the house to the kitchen where she looks at the calendar that hangs next to a cork message board that is attached to the wall next to the wall-mounted Touchtone Princess phone, cast in clear plastic, the kind they said only telephone executives (or their friends) are supposed to get. Looking at the calendar hanging on the kitchen wall Patty Duke Astin doesn't see the F-15 that screams over the back lawn in pursuit of the Russian fighter-bomber. It is May 22. Patty Duke Astin is frightened. Her husband, actor John Astin, known best for his portrayal of Gomez in the situation comedy The Addams family, is on location shooting an episode of Fantasy Island. Patty Duke Astin will be alone for the end of the world, and even though she is frightened, Patty Duke Astin knows she will survive. Patty Duke Astin remembers the prophecy. "The Americans who survive will be the spiritual leaders in the new civilization." Patty Duke Astin knows what she will become after the coming end of the world. Patty Duke Astin will be a priestess in the new order. The new world will need Americans if it is to transform into America, will need Americans to interpret the signs that will be left behind. Even the Canadians with all their newly acquired space will want to be Americans, and thus need Americans to hasten the changes. Patty Duke Astin will welcome the new world. It will be a wonderful world. We will worship in 2 car garages, Patty Duke Astin thinks. The old temples will be defunct, or become hotels, or mausoleums. Or restaurants. Or simply destroyed. Patty Duke Astin looks around her, at her modern kitchen, surveying the icons of the coming new world. Cuisinart, can-opener, microwave oven. Far off, Patty Duke Astin can hear the nuclear destruction of Los Angeles. The floor begins to shake but Patty Duke Astin is no longer afraid. Patty Duke Astin lived through starring in the movie version of The Valley of the Dolls. Patty Duke Astin is a survivor. Patty Duke Astin freshens her cup of coffee for perhaps the last time from the pot sitting on her Mister Coffee warming tray. Patty Duke Astin smiles.

-=-

To save time, list the implications. The government prefers long lines, particularly in its poetry. The hint of a link between scarcity and scansion comes clear as it all goes on sale. Image and nation linked in economics even though the money isn't what it used to be. Or what it claims to be. You could write things like you don't know me. Not really. Or you don't need me and the sky might suddenly be clear, the air clean and endless like today. The moment might pass obviously, like a car or a flock of geese in an early October evening. You'd reach for a pen the way in a different time someone might have reached for a gun. The act of writing as an act of self-defense. The letters of rejection that might or might not accumulate would simply say that there is no funding available for your project at this time, and if there was, it wouldn't be enough. You might smile. At any rate you'd still be writing. An endless, as they say, cycle.

=-=

Canned chances (MD/mjb)

     I have forced myself to contradict myself in order to avoid conforming to my own taste. –Marcel Duchamp

Glimpses of the snippets of light.

My intention was always to get away from myself, though I know perfectly well I was using myself. –M. D.

Transformative value.

I saw her from time to time, but I never talked to her. It didn't even occur to me to talk to her. I didn't even know her name. –M. D.

On a subway in in spring, I watch her across the aisle. As we scoot under Boston, she declines my offer for a drink. When I tell the story of this brief interlude on the BMT, I will still go glassy as if we'd shared a glance across the rims of our wine glasses.

The dead should not be permitted to be so much stronger than the living. We must learn to forget the past, to live our own lives in our own times. –M. D.

& looking at the Large Glass, I stop.
& looking at the Swift Nudes, I stop.
& looking at LHHOQ, I stop.
The 3 standard stoppages.
& I go on.

Every word I tell you is false and wrong. –M. D.

Her white face.
Eros is the life.
Her white face.

Eros c'est la vie.
Her white face.
Rrose Sélavy.

Or inside room. In sight room. Painting. Panting. Parting, towards silence. Then action. Full lives of insignificance raised to art. In advance of the broken arm, rules fall before tools. Intentions. I seek a quiet time, of seclusion, void of meaning. Landscapes lean toward equity. Postcards. Meaninglessness. A truer topic with a readymade rebuttal – But this isn't seeing...this is seeing! Is it possible to argue both remarks as a conceptual justification?

Humor and laughter – not necessarily derogatory and derision – are my pet tools. This may come from my general philosophy of never taking the world too seriously—for fear of dying of boredom. –M. D.

& s/he didn't like it. & didn't get, & may never get it or like it. Mutual consent/singular regret. (?) Bricks. "It's a man's world," he sang. Bats. Buts. A but. Meant.

Art is all a matter of personality. –M. D.

=-=

Wesley is sitting at a window after supper. As I go into the room I wonder if he is looking outdoors or at his reflection. He is talking to himself. "When shuh mir be all thrum sheslurl...

plane." I lean over him to look into the darkening sky. "Do you see a plane, Wes?" Wesley looks up at me with the look teachers used to give when I'd make a stupid guess at an answer, and he makes it clear that if I'm to be the receiver of a 2 year old's insight into the workings of the world, I'd best be quiet. "No plane. Nah neh shri run not real plane." He reaches for a bird watcher's guide that hangs by the window, or maybe it was sitting on a table or a radiator below the window. "She noh noneh whee nirl shut not real birds." I turn to Bill who's come into the room and is standing behind us. "So he's figured out that we talk in sentences," I say, and Bill answers, "Yeah, and he already knows the trick of filling in the blanks of what he doesn't know with noise that sounds like he does." Wesley smiles at Bill, and the three of us laugh.

-=-

From Boys Will Be Boys

So it's Bill walking four paces in front of me with Betty on his arm, or it's Jack walking four paces in front of me with Betty on his arm, or it's Dick walking four paces in front of me with Betty on his arm. It's all the same to me you see. And to you. You hardly notice me anyway, lugging all this camera stuff around behind this guy and his latest girl Friday. So we're walking down the street and a black sedan pulls into an open parking space just down the street ahead of us, and all we can do is keep walking towards it, Betty maybe holding onto Bill's arm a little tighter, or Jack's arm a little tighter, or Dick's arm a little tighter, those long nails of hers digging through the gray fabric of his suit into his arm, and Bill turns and gives me a quick high sign, or Jack turns and gives me a quick high sign, or Dick turns and gives me a quick high sign, and I fall back even a little further behind them trying to slip some of my camera stuff off my shoulder and onto the sidewalk, and start getting ready to take a shot. The door of the sedan opens and this good-looking babe steps out all in this tight red outfit with a stole, a real mink stole like out of the movies draped around these swell shoulders, and she flashes a nyloned gam, no wait, it's an incredible silked gam she flashes at us, and she kind of folds out of the door of that sedan into a sashaying step past the two of them, and says over her shoulder, "Here I open a parenthesis about what I think of Jean Luc Godard," and she goes into the building we're all standing in front of, the doorman trying so hard not to stare as she goes by, looking to heaven once she's gone and whistling for deliverance, and the babe's driver is standing by the open door of the sedan, wiping at a spot on the fender and smiling, just smiling. And Bill and Betty, or Jack and Betty, or Dick and Betty are standing in the middle of the sidewalk staring at each other like a pair of offended Puritans, and then he turns to me and says, "Did you get a load of that, Flash?", or he says, " Did you get a load of that, Toots?", or he says, "Did you get a load of that?, Hap?" and I look back at him, fumbling with the camera, dropping a lens, wrapping a ribbon of exposed film around myself like an idiot and I answer, "Yeah, well Bill, I just snaps 'em, or I say, "Yeah, well Jack, I just snaps 'em," or I say, "Yeah, well

Dick, I just snaps 'em," and screw up my face like some dufus and smirk. Just then a kid comes running past me. Grimy
t-shirt, khakis, baseball cap. "Easy, punk," I snap, or "Easy,
pal," I whine, or "Easy, kid," I mutter, cradling my camera
like a newborn as he bumps my shoulder. The kid stops in
front of Betty and her guy breathless. Betty gasps, "Ricky!",
too surprised to be put off by his scruffy look. "What's the
matter?" "Betty, ya gotta help me! I needa match." A wild-
eyed look over his shoulder through me and back down the
street. She reaches for his shoulder, then pulls back her hand,
sniffing at his shirt. "Is that gas? Ricky, you're too young to
smoke. What do you nee-..." Ricky cuts her short. "Come
on, Sis! I need a match Are you go—," and Bill or Jack or
Dick steps between them. "I'll handle this, Betty," he says, a
cigarette in his mouth, lighter in his hand. The kid's eyes go
wide like a wino facing Tokay, and Bill misreads the look, or
Jack misreads the look, or Dick misreads the look, and turns
on the charm. "What's this all about, Rick?" He glares down
my look of warning. "What do you need a match for?" He's
so confident, he falls like a redwood when the kid lands a fist
on his jaw. Betty watches me watch the punk grab the lighter
and run off. Betty and me kneel beside Mr. Cool and Calm
Reporter, and help him to his feet. "You sure don't take a
punch like a newspaperman, Ace" I say. "Lucky punch,
Flash," he says, rubbing his jaw, or "Lucky punch, Toots,"
he says, rubbing his jaw, or "Lucky punch, Hap," he says,
rubbing his jaw. A fire truck, siren blaring, rushes past. Betty
sniffs delicately. "Do you smell smoke?" We watch the fire

truck race towards the pillars of smoke that are rising at the end of the street. Flames are leaping from three pyres in the intersection, drawing pedestrians past us to them. A notebook appears in Bill's or Jack's or Dick's hand. "Let's earn our dough," they all yell and Betty stops short, screaming "RICKY!!" The kid is sitting in the intersection, a bus slamming its brakes and coming to a stop in from him. The kid tosses his gas can at it, and it rolls to a stop under the front bumper. He flips open Bill's lighter, or he flips open Jack's lighter, or he flips open Bill's lighter. The doorman is tapping me on the shoulder. "Do you smell gas?" More fire trucks are wailing down the street. Across the street a couple of kids holding hands are leaving the intersection, walking in the opposite direction. From a radio above us some other kids are screaming what sounds like "This is the Modern World, This Modern World" at us from the future. In the middle of the intersection, a huge black and red rose explodes into the afternoon out of Ricky's back. A woman is screaming on the sidewalk. Her tall, good-looking newspaperman-type boyfriend is supporting her. They watch the explosion steady into a single flame which feeds this fourth pyre that is rising into the afternoon. Behind us, the woman in red leaves the building she had entered, and walks across the sidewalk to the black sedan. She turns to me and says, "Here I close a parenthesis about what I think of Jean Luc Godard." The door of the sedan closes, and the car pulls away, weaving through the smoking obstacles in the intersection. The man and woman are still staring at the woman's brother who is sitting cross-legged in the middle of the intersection burning. "This is where we call it a day, Ace," I say, and drop the camera to the sidewalk behind them. I head for a phone booth, drop in a dime, and dial the number. The phone on the other end of the line ringing, I look back at the joker still standing there on the sidewalk with the broad. 'Sorry, Bill," I say, or "Sorry, Jack", or "Sorry, Bill, but this one's mine." "City Desk," a voice says down the line. "This is Roscoe," I say. "Whatta ya mean, Roscoe who? Listen, call me Flash. Or Toots. Or Hap. Or Mopsy. Yeah, that's me. Yeah, seen me all those years and never knew my name, right? Well, it's Karns, Roscoe Karns. Stop the presses. Have I got a story for you."

-=-

It was like a moment from the handbook of approach and avoidance motivation. Something that unprecedented, yet still accommodated. Or so we thought. Compassion and self-hate as gardening might be a possible alternative to whatever color schemes for the unbelievable interiors that will become available for reutilization. As these known worlds become apparent, the manual suggests looking for similarities. Life amidst sniper fire and artillery barrages on the civilian population varies from culture to culture…not, even as people run for cover and call out for emergency teams in 72 different languages, all the while wishing the matter had been discussed at town meeting, even as an unaddressed agenda item for later in the transcript. If only there'd been a workshop, or a segment on Across the Fence. She was singing some old song, reaching for the bottle of gin as if we were in a movie, and not a meeting. The minutes reflect it was something about appraisals and aspidistras. A curious moment had arrived that seemed Orwellian almost in its profundity and incredible lack of tact. Someone suggests turning down the record player, and a Dolphy solo slips off into the afternoon, replaced by a blast of static as the conference call begins. Pens skitter across notebooks and fingers fly across keyboards as a voice someplace else says we're all connected, and that today we'll be talking about the unparalleled by-products of the information industry and their implications for the revival of leisure time. Next up: Cooking replacing cookery as simultaneously a sense of accomplishment in the renaming of the everyday options is encouraged.

=-=

...Malik anticipates a future much like the present. No good, no evil, just lots of participation with no actual involvement with results. In the end, nothing will be at stake. We'll still fall in love, he writes, or be in love or out of love or falling out of love, living our lives and watching the sun rise and fall as the meetings go on and on. The vagaries of our expertise will still exemplify our various limitations, our various agendas, balancing the influence of our wants with their needs.

-=-

He reads a story called George Grosz while listening to a piece of music entitled John Milton.

THIS IS MY LATEST STORY

It's 3:30. A Wednesday. Late afternoon. i'm in bed. The cat's sleeping at my feet. The clock, a jet in the distance, Eb's even breathing the sounds in the room. Sometimes I can hear a car out on the road. i've taken the day off to keep the heating pad on these muscles that i strained in my back yesterday. The kids downstairs just got home so i have to finish this story quick. i've been reading a book about world war 3 which makes me want to finish another story i'm working on, a piece called "Search and Destroy." I've also been looking at photographs of the Italian artist Piero Manzoni in a book on Conceptual Art. 1 photo is captioned "Piero Manzoni showing one copy of his multiple edition of Merda d'artista, 1961." He's standing in a bathroom holding up a specimen jar with a stool floating in it. Another caption reads, "Manzoni making artist's breath," and he's blowing up a balloon, and in turn he reminds me of an article that i want to quote by Victor Burgin, an English conceptualist. i'll put it in when I type this up. "Some recent art has tended to take its essential form in message rather than in materials. In its logical extremity this tendency has resulted in placing art within the linguistic infrastructure which previously served merely to support art." There. I almost forgot to tell you – this morning I wrote another story. i call it Longish Lines. It's a concrete fable, or maybe a punch-line à la Gertrude Stein. It's pretty basic, and there's the feel of a tape loop to it. Like Brian Eno. Like the Evening Star record. Or the Discreet Music record that's on now. Longish Lines is almost a discreet story. Anyway, it's time to wrap this up, and get a little more reading in before Linda gets home. In the little pile by the bed is a copy of Wolfgang Borchert's Sad Geraniums, Richard Kostelanetz' Breakthrough anthology and Roland Barthes by Roland Barthes. Also Roland Barthes' Pleasures of the Text, which for no reason i will open and quote at random. "However, if one were to manage it, the very utterance of drifting today would be a suicidal discourse." That's a little bleak. How about this instead, the preceding sentences: "Drifting occurs whenever social language fails me. Thus another name for drifting would be: the intractable – or perhaps even stupidity." So it's 3:50 and that's it. 500 words and about 20 minutes of a day off spent mostly in bed that i call This Is My Latest Story.

=-=

I'm much happier reading than writing.
—Roberto Bolaño

So many people do this better than me, and some of you are listening to this right now even as I write that. I imagine that's why I have so many books in the house, and why I discover another new favorite writer to investigate almost every day. This is only partly because of my job at the library, and might also explain why I can't sustain a piece of writing for any serious amount of time. Like now. This paragraph (and it certainly wasn't conceived as anything more than a paragraph that might be upgraded later to a prose poem with

the addition of a metaphor, or an allusion, or a little bit of
value-added language) was originally going to be a rumination on the French author Jules Renard. Two recent translations of his Natural Histories have come into the library this
summer, and the introduction to one of them alludes to his
journals which we don't own in translation, so I've ordered
a copy for the collection. In the meantime, the author of the
introduction mentions Julian Barnes' discussion of Renard
in his memoir Nothing to be Frightened Of, so of course I
went upstairs to look at it, and discovered that Barnes' book
is something I really should read. And even as I want to be
writing this description of a digression, I get distracted by
photographs of the landscapes of the Yangtze River while
cataloging In the Footsteps of Augustine Henry, wonderfully
evocative pictures of fog and cliffs, the flowing waters of the
Yangtze River, the fauna of the Three Gorges Region, finally
the simple magic summoned just by typing the words "Three
Gorges Region" a second time. And then of course, not out
of the blue as I first started to write but very much out of my
memory comes this image of coming around or over a hill up
in Orleans County years ago and getting that first glimpse
of Lake Willoughby, or just there, the sight of the hills along
I-89 that snowy, foggy afternoon, the light almost gray, blur-
ring the trees into stark Chinese drawings that floated along-
side us as I rode up to St.Johnsbury with Bud in that boat of a
car he used to drive when we went up to listen to ... to ... to
Tom Raworth read at the Atheneum in front of that wonderful Bierstadt painting of Yosemite Valley. Tom Raworth who

I'm sure didn't read How to Patronize a Poem that night, the poem where he writes "Do you see me? / I am leaving a space / where I was / is as bad." ...Another of those writers who does this so much better than me.

"I don't have to leave my house to see the world," Roberto Bolaño says the Tao Te Ching says. There's a copy of the Tao Te Ching around here someplace, so I should probably go dig it out and see if I can find a context for that sentence. Maybe I will later, but for now I've got something else I'd like to talk about. Pop would have been 85 last Thursday. He died April 12, 2000. I've written about him a few times since he died, and I was thinking about reading a couple of those pieces in his memory tonight, but then I remembered a poem I'd written back in the 70's that I thought I'd read instead. But when I went searching for it and finally found it, I was a little disturbed by the poem. Although there are a couple of nice lines, for the most part it's a fairly dishonest bit of maudlinism (I was hoping maudlinousity might be a word but I'm afraid it's not.) So instead of reading the poem, I'll just share the introduction for it that I came up with. One afternoon when I was in college, when my father and I had reached a truce in our long struggle over the Vietnam war and the state of the Union (another story), I went over to the house to help him put new tarpaper on the back roof. A nasty job. He'd already taken up the old paper and replaced some of the old flashing with new metal (aluminum?) sheets. (A little aside here – one of the first times I brought Linda over to the house, Pop excused himself from the room and went out to the garage. He came back with one of those aluminum sheets. He told us he got them from the Free Press and that they were the sheets that were used for printing the paper. And apparently, my father would read each of the sheets before he used them, as this sheet was page 3 of the Burlington Free Press dated Thursday, May 11, 1972. The headline at the top of the page reads 51 Arrested at Federal Building Keep Judges Busy. In the body of the article Linda is listed as one of the 3 students who pleaded nolo condentere to the charge of obstructing pedestrian traffic. I'm looking at this metal sheet as I type, pondering the tangle of chance that got it from the Free Press printing rooms to my Father's hands and then on to Linda's, and now here to this page, and closing this aside.) Anyway, a nasty job. A hot sunny day in a string of hot sunny days which is the only time you do a job like putting on a new roof, and my father and I have declared a truce and we're together on the back roof, and he looks across the roll of tarpaper we have stretched between us and, wiping away the sweat rolling down his forehead, he says to me, in the only line of that dishonest poem that you're going to hear, "Do good so's you'll never have to live like this," and he smiles at me and I smile at him and nod and we get back to nailing new tarpaper on the back roof. Eventually of course we didn't need a truce to see each other. To paraphrase Joe Strummer's Clampdown, we grew up and we calmed down and I got married and we became friends again, and the years went by, and then he had cancer, and he died in about 6 weeks, and I often wonder how he would have reacted to the 21st century and what's become of us all. I've got this idea for a book that I'd like to write if I could write the kind of book it would probably have to be. It would be called September 10, and it would be some kind of digressive monologue based around the front pages of various newspapers from that day and the days previous to it. A different world in many ways, the book would be a monologue based on my father's world.

-=-

Someplace in the building a drill is working, but by the time the sound makes it to the keyboard and this page, it's a fog horn, plaintive, distant, enhancing the random almost silence of the unlistened-to recording slipping out of the headphones lying on my desk. The first impulse is rewrite, to issue a summoning call for poetry, a salvage operation based around the image when, as if in response, or maybe that's mockery, a generator rumbles on outside. It seems we are surrounded by imagery this morning, just as we are on any morning, even though that generator continues on untransformed and metaphor free. To discern, to describe, takes time, time away from the job at hand. A poetics of the workspace might be called theft. Now a printer whines, and there is something so unreal in the microcosm. Perhaps it is merely the allure of fiction, the story. The lamentation that rises as the CD comes to an end. Perhaps an explication of memory, of allegory, might suffice. You think Muezzin, you think museum, then you write mezzanine. The recoded recording as you stare into the afternoon sky reflected in a room divider. A cloud observed moving along the tree line. If there is a simulacrum to be found here, which is most real – this page, this room, or that unrecorded conversation? All are simple environments, or so we hope. Another printer groans into operation, and more trees surrender to others' words. The goal is a focal point, the dream of return. Pictures fade, and you lick your wounds. Domestic? Feral? Is this barking up the wrong tree, or howling at the moon? And do either of these reflect the moment? Later you will read: Art: That's the problem with Art. You could call it waiting, copying the line into your notebook, recalling virtually every conversation you've had with writers and artists who insist the problem is something different. There will be peace one day, and sleep. This will finally be a version of leisure, a vision of work, but not now. For now, there is silence, a secret for another time. For now, this flailing about in our stupid sheltered lives is our stupid sheltered life. For now the car bombs that really matter to us are so far away, even further than beyond our allies' burning doctors and SUVs. For now, it's overheating and overeating. For now, ring tones are the latest expression of personal statements. For now, there is the random silence of the unlistened-to recording. And someplace there is the memory of a performance, the quick and mysterious efficiency of the pianist, her hands a gentle hammering across the keyboard. There is the cellist, the viola player, the manic mannerisms of the violinist, vague memories undefined until recalled, written down, the light falling away through the windows, beyond a dog straining at the leash, belying the calm of the tableau.

=-=

Tempered by circumstance

"Somebody else's idea of somebody else's world is not my idea of things as they are."
—Sun Ra

A beautiful Saturday morning here on the porch in West Roxbury. A soft breeze rattling loose dry leaves under a sky as blue as a faded work shirt and as pointless as an egg we watched someplace else roll slowly down another driveway until it came to a stop in another street. What do I tell you – That Steve died the day before we got here? That I didn't say goodbye? That we watch the emotions flash across Jo's face as she tells stories of the last days? The last breath, the last words, that 2 times towards the end Steve referred to someone called "The Man" who sounded like Pop, whom Steve never met? The last time he got into bed? This is certainly someone else's story I want to tell, moments caught by another. Meanwhile, 500 hundred miles to the south, a one-eyed red-tailed hawk sits in a cage watching squirrels feed on the sidewalk before her. A hundred miles to the northeast, sandpipers race across the wet sand of a Maine beach behind the receding tide. In 4 days, 217 miles to the northwest I will read "I remember when polio was the worst thing in the world," a line from Joe Brainard's I Remember that I linked to in Bill's room. And here, as I type, I listen to Jane Siberry singing the line "This ain't the fading of the light" in her song Goin' Down the River, and back there, on the deck in West Roxbury that Steve took to calling "the Pirate Ship," I stand leaning against the railing. A single cloud lolls off the horizon and into the morning. Buds sit at the ends of branches of the dwarf Japanese blood maple, waiting for winter, and beyond, the chance to open in May. And I see Steve's eyes pop open the way they would, in a kind of bemused amazement.

=-=

It's the middle of the last century, and too many people think they're living in the future. Almost as many as those who think they're still living in the past. There's a war on and our country is probably fighting it, so who can be sure who was correct? There's no Internet yet, not even in science fiction. There's barely cable television, although my dad, one of the great unsung technophiles of the aforementioned last century, got it as soon as it was affordable for a mailman living in Burlington, Vermont with 3 kids and a mortgage. Watching They Were Expendable when it was broadcast by WMTW from Poland Springs, Maine in 1964 was a formative event in your author's life. While watching the movie FM radio is still in the future. I won't know what album rock even is for almost half a decade, but I'll know who Lloyd Thaxton is before I know where Vietnam is. I'm writing this as I look at the photograph on the cover of Michael Brownstein's Strange Days Ahead, the book that is sitting just above the keyboard as I type, and I'm wondering (no, hoping) that the picture is only a cliché because I'm bringing it to your attention as I write this paragraph. The 3 farmers going to a dance were photographed by August Sanders about 50 years before the time I'd like you to start thinking about. And of course we might be 40 or 50 years on from the time I'd like to talk about, which is an irony I might want to get back to a little later on. The series of photographs the photograph was taken from was entitled People of the 20th Century. Some really amazing work. As are the poems that comprise Michael Brownstein's book, which was published in 1975, which is a year that from here might be considered as a part of the era under consideration. This of course feels like a bit of a stretch for those of us who lived during this period, but again, maybe that's something for us to talk about another time. Let's just say that this time thing is something I'm more than a little intrigued by. The influence of our pasts on what's left of the present now, and the future that is ahead of us. For now, let's consider this a kind of introduction, a tentative first step. After all, as someone once said, this is just writing.

=-=

Oh, Chloe Caldwell, author of Legs Get Led Astray, I love you or your back cover blurb writer…what else is there to do but quote when you write — "Bookstore crushes."

-=-

Like a tourist you discover a need for a perceptual record of where you are, of what you see. But you think that you can't just take snapshots, as that would make you look like a tourist, like the ugly American. So you must study composition, master dark room techniques, learn the subtleties of working with black and white. You've yet to learn that the snapshot is once in a lifetime, and the photograph is just another page in the history book. Even now, here in a brief excursion like this paragraph. An afternoon drive of an exercise. An onion of a drive of random turns onto dirt roads, the discovery and exploration of another world here in your world. The next morning there is a flurry of motion just there of the edge of sight as herons take flight at the far end of a marsh you drive past every morning. You pull the car over to watch the herons fly off, the slow push for altitude, strain concealed in motion and distance, effortlessness only a point of view as they disappear above the trees. You might snap a picture, or if there's time and you've got the skills, you might take a photograph. Either way the end product is a blur of greys and dull blues and greens. It ends up in an envelope that travels with you from home to home. Years later you come across the envelope and see the photograph. It triggers a memory. The morning returns. Herons are flying across the ceiling. Your words follow them. And while you sit thinking of this other world, something in your body lets go, a muscling tightening at the back of your neck, or a wild drumming above your lungs as if a bird were trying to escape from your ribcage, a reminder from your body of who is in control, of that other world there below the brain, of that other world that keeps us in touch with everything out there, out here.

=-=

Can we talk about a man who is sitting in his living room?
A man sitting in a chair his wife has reupholstered herself,
listening to his not inexpensive sound system. Mozart, Miles,
whatever. His reading music, most likely. Smoking his pipe,
an after dinner bowl of his special blend as he reads a magazine. Or maybe a book. A good book, and not a bestselling
good book, a classic, maybe a contemporary classic. He looks
up as the whine of a jet becomes just a bit louder than usual,
growing louder and louder, growing to a roar, the room filling with the booming rush of sound. He looks past his wife
who is sitting in a chair in his line of sight, past the curtains

that his wife made and hung herself, past the array of plants, each of which is named and cared for, the plants that sit in the window greenhouse that he and his wife built themselves, past the well-kept front lawn that he cuts and waters every Saturday morning, and he sees the jet coming out of the sky and not just out of the sky but directly at him. Can we talk about this man, his attention slowly being pulled from the jet that is soon to shatter the window he is watching it through, and not just through the window but the wood and stone and metal that surrounds him, protects him as well, his attention shifting to his wife, the woman that he loves so deeply, all of his attention left to a glance, years of devotion, of caring, of loving left to a glance as she raises her gaze to his as she and he and everything are to be joined in a few moments to a crashing jet and oblivion. Can we say that what he feels is really an overwhelming sense of unfairness? I think not.

-=-

With the acceleration towards silence, the words can only lose meaning even as they accumulate. Eventually they slip away, leaving the moment, the story, to fend for itself.

-=-

One of those odd moments of juxtaposition, walking down a hallway in a research center, the research center in a good-sized university, and the air is pretty bad, that sort of closed up building and sweat and chemicals and who knows what else sort of stink that a lot of us have learned to live with. Let's call it something unoriginal like the stink of the modern. Anyway, you're walking down this hallway and not really noticing "the stink of the modern" as you're conversing about something humanistic with your companion. Maybe nuclear disarmament, or liberation theology or a single payer health plan. Maybe it's about aid to the Contras, or the embargo on Iraqi airspace, or the gubernatorial race, anyway something timely and important and you find yourself walking past a cage sitting in the hallway and you notice a research animal sitting there, a rodent, a hamster maybe, or a rat. Its feeding bin is filled with food (Purina hamster chow, or some organic alternative) and the little guy is sucking on a little tube on his water bottle, just as if those leads stuck in his head (or her head) didn't cause any discomfort, and of course maybe they don't since they're not hooked up to any wires or machines, And you just look at this rodent in this cage and you walk on as your companion talks about unionizing or getting people to vote and you're not wondering what the world would be like if you weren't humanists.

=-=

This story is happening back when spit-flavored ice cream was all the rage. [See how that happened? 14 words and we already know the story is being told in a future where spit-flavored ice cream may or may not be almost nostalgic. Sorry for the interruption. I won't be back] It's a beautiful late summer evening and Jeannine is enjoying a spit-flavored ice cone as she sits on the front stoop with her children Adrian and Leila. As they enjoy their ice cream cones, simple rewards they have given themselves for the arduous day's work that they each put in at the "parking garage" where they all work together as a happy, harmonious and industrious family unit, Jeannine is telling Adrian and Leila about the ice cream flavors she remembers from when she was a little girl. Right now she is telling them about the heavenly hash of her youth, a rich combination of nuts, chocolate chunks, marshmallow, caramel swirls and who can remember what all else. Adrian and Leila can see the rapturous look on their mother's face as she tells her story and can only begin to imagine what the flavors of these mysterious ingredients she's talking about must have tasted like. Adrian and Leila have never seen or tasted chocolate or caramel or marshmallow or even peanuts, let alone walnuts, crushed or otherwise. And now she is telling them that when she was their age, before she went to high school, and then on to college and graduate school, and became an electrical engineer, and met a man she fell in love with until he died after he had helped her start a family and before everything went south to hell, and much later when she found work at the "parking garage" [which of course isn't really a parking garage anymore and why the words parking garage are in quotes but you really don't want to know what they do there now. That's another story. Sorry. I felt I had tolet you in on that fact. This time I mean it. I won't be back], and she turned that entry level position at the "parking garage" into a little family enclave, that when she was almost there someone had told her about the old-fashioned way ice cream makers would make heavenly hash. How at the end of the day or the end of the week, frugal cost-efficient ice cream makers would gather up bits of chocolate and vanilla ice cream, caramel swirl, chocolate chunks and so on, combine them is a single tub and sell what was there as heavenly hash. "Of course, that was a long time ago, in the days of ice cream parlors, before Heavenly Hash got branded and standardized," Jeannine said, finishing her little reverie with some of that dead language she sprinkled her stories with, and leaned back there on the front stoop and took a lick of her spit-flavored ice cream cone. Adrian and Leila smiled at the conclusion of their mother's story and like her they leaned back, licking their spit-flavored ice cream cones. It would seem they made a lovely picture of familial bliss sitting there almost picture perfect on the front stoop and licking their spit-flavored ice cream cones. All we need now is a photographer from the city's local paper to drive by, spot them, stop his car, take their picture and we might find it on the front page of tomorrow's paper's local section: a picture with some catchy title and the caption Jeannine and her children Adrian and Leila enjoy their spit-flavored ice cream cones and the beautiful sunset after an honest day's work at the "parking garage". But of course there is no local paper, there is no photographer, and there is no beautiful sunset, but that's the way the moment felt even as Jeannine arched her back a bit further, cleared her throat and spat mightily against the wall of their apartment building. "That's all that's left," she said as the great gob of spittle crawled down the wall as angry and obvious as the sun crawling toward the horizon to the west, "that's heavenly hash."

-=-

In a notebook he reads "Existing is plagiarism" and can't remember where he copied it from. [Google moment — Emil Cioran] The phone rings. A voice asks, "Have you ever really looked carefully at your watch?" You put the phone on the counter. You have nothing to say to Bertolt Brecht. Besides, your watch is missing. There's a gap in the conversation. You need your watch. Now the phone dangles from the edge of the counter. It's time to go. Something as stupid as something from Kafka. You want to be modern. You want to be "up to date." You think about dying and think that it's the same as thinking about being killed. The phone rings. There is no one there when you finally answer. Who replaced the phone? You open your eyes. Something as stupid as something from Kafka. You wake up, and remember you don't have a phone. You have a clock radio. You stare at the green numerals displayed by your clock radio, as it groans on about an explosion in El Salvador. The station fades out. You blink your eyes. You wake up again. You're thinking about wrist watch radios, wrist watch telephones. You smile. Something as stupid as something from Kafka. You're in the bath room, and a German accented voice from the vanity asks, "Haf you ever looked carefully at your vatch?" Cold water is running over a washcloth. You turn off the water, wring the water from the cloth. In the apartment next door the telephone is ringing. You put the washcloth to the back of your neck. The phone is still ringing, just like in the dream and you think that you understand the dream. It is suddenly as clear as really looking carefully at your watch, but hearing the telephone ringing in the apartment next door is not the same as hearing the telephone ringing in your apartment in a dream, and you see that this is nothing like really looking carefully at your watch. You don't have a watch. The telephone in the apartment next door is still ringing. Your lover's digital watch is sitting on the tank of the toilet. 5:58, it says. 2/18. It says 5:58, 2/18. 5:58, 2/18, 5:58, 2/18. 5:58/, 2/18 it says again in a steadying sort of steady way, and it say 5:59, 2/18 and you think you understand the dream about a voice on a telephone asking about a watch, as if the voice was interested in your lover's digital watch, and not your watch. The telephone stops ringing in the apartment next door as if to confirm your thinking. A rivulet of water from the washcloth runs down your back along your spine. The clock radio is talking about a watch factory in Korea. The telephone is ringing again. You hear yourself waking up again on the radio. The telephone next door is ringing again on the radio. Cold water is running over a washcloth again. You turn off the water again, wring the water from the cloth again, and put the washcloth to the back of the radio. Something as "stupid" as something from Kafka. Your neighbor is hammering on the wall. Your neighbor is asking you what time it is. Someone on the radio is describing the future as someplace where there in nothing but everything that is left to happen. You close your eyes. You open your eyes. The window is open, and your neighbor is leaning into the room with his telephone in his hand, saying it's for you. Something as stupid as something from Kafka. Time to go. You turn to leave, and your lover is standing in the doorway staring at your wrist, and asks, "Have you ever really looked carefully at your watch?

=-=

One day to be cataloging Edward Lucie-Smith's Lives of the Great Artists of the 20th Century, and come across a picture of Joseph Beuys "action" How to Explain Paintings to a Dead Hare and then trying to explain the tears that are trailing down my cheeks. To have this culture of death and dying set up and exposed again at my workstation this Tuesday morning, something lovely in the headphones and a cup of coffee within reach. What to do but record it? And later, in the reading of the entry, to recall sitting with Jim in Nector's one night as he tells us about his bypass and its aftermath, and the doctors told him to expect some unexpected emotional shifts, what the doctors called mood lability and I smiled and put an arm his shoulder and asked, "Did they tell you how to spot the difference?"

=-=

On the other side of Rock City Falls, rte. 29 comes out of the forested foothills and heads down into a cleared valley. As we drive, Neil Tennant is singing, "What have I, what have

I, what have I done to deserve this?" and there sitting above the horizon is a burnished aluminum colored cloud with a fluffy white border sitting in a clear blue sky. To the right of us a largish wetland spiked with a seemingly endless number of dead trees slides past. Later on, an intersection with a road that could take us to the Great Sacandaga Lake, and even further on, a solitary figure stands on a hill tracking us as he watches the world go by on this state highway. Finally, a Teen War is happening Saturday night at an evangelical church, and Neil Tennant sings again, "Someone told me Monday, someone told me Saturday, Wait until tomorrow and there's still no way. Read it in a book or write it in a letter, wake up in the morning and there's still no guarantee," as we slow at the Johnstown town line, merge onto 30A, and head for the entrance ramp to the Northway.

-=-

She takes my DVDs, smiling at the previous customer's baby who is still smiling at the cashier, looking back over her mother's shoulder, and says, mixing our exchange into the long mix of her shift, "wouldn't it be great to be young again?" and turning back to me with her non-ending smile. I smile back trying not to look at her bad teeth, looking for something to say and settling on a chuckled "maybe if I could bring some of this life back with me." "Oh sure, but not everything, that's for sure," she replies, scanning in my sale. "$12.93. I mean if I went back and told 'em about the twin towers, they'd think I was crazy. $2.07's your change. Then again," as she bags my DVDs and hands them to me, "maybe it would've kept us out of this terrible war," and I smile my agreement. "Thanks for coming to Wal-Mart," she says, turning her attention and smile to the next face in the long mix of her shift.

=-=

Another certainty. That the hope is to re-start not simply re-state. When the landscape is as barren as the language used to describe it, no good can come. Consider full shelves and empty pages. Or new story, know story. She looks up from her paperwork, and asks. "Oh you write? Might I have read some of your work?", and you smile and swallow your first four answers. The secret – there is a writer at work here, not an author. For now, the words accumulate. There is no truth to be found here, only observation and obfuscation. How's this for an alternative history – imagine listening to What's Going On and Astral Weeks side to side to side to side in the fall of 1971, and then consider how much different your life might have been.

-=-

I want to stop writing but I can't. I've just written the perfect ending for a poem but it's sitting on the table crying because I don't have time to put it together with the rest of the poem that is sitting on the other end of the table in a pile of drafts of poems I've been working on. And this situation is starting to feel like an old Fleischer cartoon. My left hand is waving like a balloon over the sheet of paper, and my left arm's gone all loose and long and rubbery and now the first part of the poem is starting to cry and it sounds like Koko the Clown and the words to the ending of the poem are jumping up and down on their page and making like they want to jump off the table. With my right hand I'm sweeping over the table looking for a pencil to salvage the poem and I look up and the mailman is staring at me through the window as she puts our mail in the mailbox. The two parts of the poems are howling louder and louder as my hand grabs a stub of pencil that's as big around as a good sized log so I hold my breath until my left arm firms up and returns to a usable state. Meanwhile the wailing words of the beginning of the poem have joined the words of the ending of the poem and they're all running around as if there's a fire drill happening on the page. With both hands I pick up the stub of pencil. The point of the lead covers the entire sheet of paper. The poem sighs as I finish the poem with a wondrous conjunctive phrase. When I lift the pencil away from the sheet of paper all that remains is a blotch of smudged graphite. All I can remember of the poem is its cries and that last contented sigh. I have since learned that dreams of obliteration are common to many creative people.

=-=

Or try this. Nothing fancy. A simple story. I was walking down the street. Just the other day. I can't let myself go back too far. I can never be too sure about the accuracy of my memory these days. Or my imagination. For about the last year and half I've been trying to avoid using either of them, as they had been both been getting me into trouble. As a result I haven't been writing too much in that time either. I seem to be suffering from what I've taken to calling the Irish Syndrome. I'd much rather be telling stories than spend time writing them down. Lots of plot, narratives, themes, things like that, but I can't be bothered with writing down the sentences, gathering them into paragraphs and pages of fiction. I'm using up my best material casually in bars, at work, in dinner conversations. Frankly, it's kinda driving me nuts. Anyway, I'm walking down the street. Just walking and watching you, listening to you. Or not. Sometimes, it's nothing but the transit from point a to point b, measuring the trip as exiting one door and entering another. That's it. A complete suspension of interaction with the world. Until that moment. One of those moments, like this moment. The moment I've come to hate, and need to relate. That wretched unbelievably almost indescribable moment when all the bittersweet, all the joy, all the poignancy, all of the incredible passion and shit of this life comes clear as you watch a kid run through traffic, or someone up ahead of you stops short and smiles and laugh for no apparent reason, or suddenly you're thinking about nights on Geelvinck Bay, about nights on the northeast coast of New Guinea, and you stand there in the street staring into space, trying to remember where or when you've heard or felt or thought that way before, but the moment passes and you shrug and you walk into the day.

Notes from the Epoch of Confusion, partly revised

Something to do with something about starting out, or over. And you're off. Or out. He had been expecting something else, something more spectacular. Or maybe it was just something more interesting that he was looking for. As peripheral as a flash of light amongst the weeds, or Walter Murphy singing Wildfire pushing out of the static driving through the Berkshires, as if these might constitute a sudden appearance of evidence. A character. Sex is, check that, this isn't 1981 anymore. Gender is unimportant. a sudden urban occurrence. A street. An afternoon. Something old fashioned. They used to call it a promenade. A crowd. A window display. An ornate exhibition from memory undescribed, just noted. But here there is a semblance of interest, a desire for an inventory, a description. An arm sheathed in some brocaded material. A bracelet. The waxen expression. A certain distain discerned in the telling. Or lilac water. But I'm not going to talk about Vivien Leigh, or even Scarlett O'Hara. Nothing from Gone with the Wind. This is about a walk in the dark, and walking into a lilac bush after a rain, blossom laden boughs heavy with moisture, hanging at eye level. This is about spring. Breezes. On another night there might be stars. A starry night. The darker greens of walks. That stereotypical Irish melody across the shadowed hills on the soundtrack. I shouldn't mention peepers. Or mists across the valley. Anticipating the moment of desire, the dissimilar reaction of desire and practice. I'm wanting to think aloud, to cut out the middleman of rumination. An air of improvisation while documenting the silence, an empty description filling in the spaces of intent, this meaningless moment of movement. How about the sound of an automobile through the wall, or the water moving through a pipe, a metaphor for the rest of the world going by, like the sound of John Cage's heart and brain. I can feel a rising anticipation. Fear like an ocean, increasing the dominion of form over content, not only hear/hear on the page or in the ear, but in the heart as well. The suddenness of discovery, of the world reopening unto itself, or the meaning of the mean, as if the Tao weren't as natural as that leaf, or this intonation of the word leaf, is the discovery that leaves us in this moment. I can remember finding scraps of paper covered with my undecipherable scrawl. Sometimes poems written in dreams and read over my shoulder, sometimes poems or stories or just random thoughts scribbled late at night or early in the morning, drunk or stoned or both or just coming awake or falling to sleep, portions of this imagination coming to the surface, recovered and lost simultaneously in my recording them. But are they lost forever or lasting forever on those scraps? As if we were telling this story over and over, a radio of an evening. Perhaps it's just another weight, another waiting, that lighthearted sense of breath returning, of being able to run free, the idea, he thought, of moving out, or moving on. A new voice, or another voice. He could add his versions to the story. He can't remember what set this off, or set this free, some note in a novel, a song, an overheard conversation. He thought of writing on, and stopped. —2-6/1983

-=-

They sing ,"Forget." They sing, "Help me find a way out of this maze." They sing, "Living in another world to you." The book before me is called The Liberty of the Imagination. A catchy title that sounds like lies here in the land of the free. Hey wait. That's only a sample. That's the tease. If you want more, you gotta buy. You gotta pay. Then fill it up. The seasonal moment. Monet winter scenes. Or cherry tomatoes, how right off the vine they taste like sunshine. Another way to end it. Replace pepper ball ordinance with cherry tomatoes and the riot squad is transformed to the Tomatina squad. Occupiers laughing and smiling for the cameras covered in the harvest as they dance before the police, shouting, "comrades, let's leave the governors to their stop gap exercises as we face an uncertain future," and hand in hand, singing songs as placards and uniforms litter the parking lot around us. For more information see: national characteristics, aesthetics, imagination, landscape.

=-=

LUCID DREAMS

i dreamt I was dreaming that Linda and i were dreaming that we were dreaming about dreaming about dreaming about Nyasaland. It was hot and dry and the sounds and smells of African wildlife were on the hot wind. i could smell pines too, very faint but very much there. i remember turning to Linda to say something about the scent of pine in our dream but i don't think i said anything. Linda was wearing a beautiful long dress of blue, green and burnt orange, what i guess i'd call an African pattern of great wide stripes of burnt orange and blue tossed with geometric patches of blue. The patches of blue smelt of wet pine.

-=-

From Domesticities

Birds are singing. The birds are always singing. The sun is out. A clear day, with the sounds of children in the air, on the breeze as they move through the trees. Linda is sunbathing in the backyard, and the present tense situation is ending as he goes inside. He's thinking about filling that hole at the bottom of the backyard. Clear days like this are for thinking about work around the house. Finally taking off the storm windows, say, or putting down a new coat of sealant on the driveway, say, or seeding that patch of bare dirt along the side of the house. Saying, you see, because there's also practicing scales on the mandolin out in the sunshine. More fun than filling that hole with stones. Piling up the stones like words. He reaches for his notebook. He writes – the words begin to pile up like stones, like voices in the air. Linda is sitting up. Watching him watching her as he leans against the window frame. The present tense situation is ending. He waves down to Linda as he pays attention to one of the voices, a wrong number in Houston. He would never walk on the moon, and was pretty sure he'd never wanted to.

=-=

Something multi-lingual. Love, say. Amour. Amore. Liebe. A present that can never leave us behind. The way gifts litter the sidewalk. Schwitters. A remembered article wrapped around a pile of chicken skin and bones, gone, ink running, spreading through fat into a new kind of presentation. The traces of an afternoon. Day to day dazed preoccupations encouraged a redoubling of effort. Something mechanical. Instructions follow. Slot A. Tab f. Insert here a moment of true feeling. Looking up from the notebook she smiles as she watches him work, the slow route of the lens, the awkward rhythm of the keyboard. You slip back refreshed into the words, contact with the outside world reestablished. Love. Lyubov. Amor. Proceed to step 4.

=-=

Another birthday. Another set of promises, of resolutions, of lies. In a notebook he reads, "for the present it seems that every writer has to make the imaginative grasp at identity for himself, and if he can find no means in his inheritance to suit him, he will have to start from scratch," and he thinks another smart kid. But then, how old is Thomas Kinsella when he writes this? He'll have to track down the book he copied the quote from. Yeats and Kinsella, he sees scrawled in even more dashed cursive beside the hard to read note-book entry. And "la lutte continue" along the bottom of the quote like an underline. A pile of stories beside the desk, and a smaller heap of poems by that. A routine of clutter and disarray might not be either. 15 minutes at the desk this afternoon. A glass of wine for its own sake. Through the window, the lilac bush spreads out low under the weight of wet snow. Learning to whisper, to maintain a certain si-lence. Fill in the ____. ____ are falling from the trees. Pop-sicles. Popsicles are falling from the trees. Parish priests are falling from the trees. Preventive airstrikes are falling beyond the trees. A probable set up. Pop tarts. Pop tarts are falling from the trees. It couldn't possibly be poems. Wrap the head in mud. Or newspapers. Each can be as effective as sand. As in head stuck in. Read, this is where I work when I'm not working. Wind songs. Folding moments. Faulting moments. Some birds in some trees are singing some songs. The beginning established. Clouding over is not the same as clouding up. Slight emotions or sliding motions. Xerox beckons. A past, the past, his past? Actually, I think he meant repaste. Dinner's on the table. Don't forget your wine glass. Oh yes. Happy birthday.

-=-

This is about…a good time. It is a good time. There's Rosalind. (We'll call her Rosalind) There's Rosalind standing on the corner. And there's Johnny. (We'll call him Johnny) There's Johnny going by in a car. And there's a radio playing. There's always a radio playing somewhere. If not on the corner or in the car, then maybe from a window 2 stories above this little moment being transcribed, or maybe even in an apartment on the other side of town. And it's always something catchy playing on the radio. Maybe something South American. Or maybe something popular from El Norte. Or maybe a song by the Beatles, back when the Beatles weren't quite the Beatles. Say You're Gonna Lose That Girl. Playing from that window open 2 stories above this little moment being transcribed. So there's Rosalind, and she's standing on the corner as Johnny passes in a car. And from a radio playing in a room with a window 2 floors above you can hear the Beatles singing You're Gonna Lose That Girl and Johnny drives right on past the corner and through the intersection without even noticing Rosalind. I forgot to tell you that they don't even know each other. Not a thing in common, and not even close to being each other's type. But this corner is a nice spot to watch the day go by, and that's a nice car Johnny is driving, and of course there's Rosalind. She's nice. . . No, there's nothing going on here. It's been done before a zillion times before. But that's okay. You're Gonna Lose that Girl. Great song, isn't it?

=-=

Dreaming about dreaming about exploring space. Or a dream of falling, of stars, a group of people floating about in tight clothing on the edge of dark abyss. "Where's my stomach?" I think to myself as I start my fall. There is a hollowness there below this thought and why do I suddenly recall last night's dream as I lie underneath the ceiling fan, listening to this piece of musical theater about Debussy? How does a trained voice create this situation that gathers these not so random words into this small but certain arrangement, wanting only to be called real, to be read, to be said aloud, days later? How, or why this dream, this memory, this moment? And then there's John Hurt sounding like Derek Jarman in his beautiful elegy to himself, his movie Blue. So sad, so said, so sorely unseen. An Irish sentence if ever I wrote one.

-=-

Someone at work jokes about the death of the word. I talk about a reading block on top of a writing block. Record reviews, a cursory glance at the headlines in newspapers and web sites…that's the extent of my reading today. He nods. The death of the word, we joke. Earlier someone had been talking about Truffaut's movie of Fahrenheit 451, wondering if anyone had been reading words on a screen. Who thought we'd stop reading books as part of the evolutionary process?

=-=

SURFACE NOISE

This could all disappear. A lobster boat coming home. Hand in hand. An aspect of tangent. A serenade at dusk. Returnable. Tangiers. Mustaffi. Mustachioed. Attached at the hub. A translucence. A line of moonlight along the water. Lights sweep across the sand as someone passes the beach behind us. A scream across the rooftops. Call it a gull. Or a cat. Brakes, further away. Around a corner somewhere up beyond the beach. Neon in the distance, a shop, a bar, a café. A second story window. A flutter of curtains, a sliver of light. Fingertips. Gone. Across the street across the sand, we could say we watched. Or were watched. She talks of antiquity. Heads rolling. An old boyfriend. Wine. A gramophone sends a

sticky serenade into the night. Her hand along your forearm.
Something old. Sarah Vaughan. Bourbon someplace. Turk-
ish Ovals, Lucky Strikes. There. On the horizon. Gaining
shape, gaining texture. East. And south. Minarets, kaftans.
The proverbial pearl of cum. Jizz, or jazz. There, from the
last building on this row of summer homes, a saxophone. Going home. Or to bed. To something. Offal, that awful smell
coming from this patch of passed and ruffled sand. Ecstasy.
That car, that building, that music, that tangent on Tangiers,
all gone in the moment simply by not bringing it up. The
moon on the water. That lobster boat. That scream. Another
one, just now. The steady motion of running lights along the
horizon. Laughter. A bonfire. Someone plucking at a guitar
on the last weekend of the summer. Alone as that couple hand
in hand passing on the beach. It could be us, it could be you.
On and on and constant. Wave. Flux. Luminescence on the
water. And maybe Ben Webster playing behind us. Something
sad. Another car past us. Laughter and something with a beat
through an open window. But we're here on the beach, and
somehow that's not enough. A question. But we're here on
the beach, and somehow that's not enough? A hand along
your forearm. Fingertips. Gone.

-=-

Backing Up, or Done

He writes that writers are, pardon the expression, cursed. Not
just cursed, but a couple of times over. First, memory. Not
that unusual. The past is something we all share, or rather, a

past, since each past is recalled from a different experience. Whoever said that history was written by the winners may have forgotten that it's read by the survivors, whatever that means. Or like the other night, one actor says to another if the living took care of each other as well as they take care of the dead maybe living would be bearable. Anyway... second curse: writers not only live their lives, they feel compelled to record and transform those lives into a writing that they then have to convince not only themselves but other people to pay attention to. We'd best not go into the whole exchange of words for money. And then there is the triple curse of words, of language that pushes the writer to the front of the room, to the typewriter, to the computer, to the notebook, to actually record these combinations of words that will please at least one's own self, if not the eyes and ears, hearts and minds of others, offering solace or consternation, derision or delight, triggering memories of moments forgotten, and bringing together our separate worlds, our separate experiences of the world, at least for a moment.

-=-

Survival

1.Talent. An arrow of uncertainty. Car-pooling. A Coltrane tune, call it Naima, running out slowly, slower. Artaud is really laughing now, as these longish revealing passages start coming. If they were words the teachers might call them sentences, paragraphs, pages. Compete this one. Copy the masters. The passion goes on in 4/4 time. Alluvial, Silurian, different names for a present tense. Evenings in the gardens of Versailles. Future spa. A roomful of light, programmed good times at a quarter a shot.

2. A Sense of Reality. Most everyone has gone home. A curlicue of smoke rising from an ashtray. Bourbon swirls through ice in a chipped glass. Flaubert is chipping at sentences now. The radio goes on and on. The first time I wrote that? Outside, a head slides across the bottom of the window. A bell rings 4 times. Nearing completion, another outsider, "a beautifully wrought book. Hecht's poems should be treated as sacred objects. Reading them tends to make other poets feel clumsy." Artaud is laughing. Shakespeare changes the channel. In the cab I'll say "Take us home," and Spicer will say, "Turn up the radio." And the colored girls sing....

3. Business Sense. Artaud shows us his novel. It is long, 1400 hundred pages of autobiographical prose. Rodez, EST, the cabbages telling him about home. We all smile, and begin reading. It takes days and days and days, going around the room, the pages, days we could have spent listening to the Beatles' Hamburg Tapes or practicing the saxophone, or writing our own novels but Artaud sits smoking an endless chain of Old Golds and sipping a bottomless quart of Miller High Life. Even with albums of gamelan music from the Nonesuch Explorer series as our soundtrack the novel stinks but we want to be good and supportive friends, and Bantam has already given Antonin a $50000 advance. Artaud says

he could have gotten more but he never got a degree. Shakespeare laughs, and says they saw him coming. As he leaves, Beethoven tells him to get an agent, the sale was a fluke.

4. Balance. Last of the spring flowers. Chaz tells us about peas, the way he loves peas. When they come in, his daughters just sit in the garden eating sweet peas right out of the pod. Typical girls. A beautiful day, sitting on the porch, a glass of chilled white wine, wheat thins, gruyere. Boys and girls playing in the street, an old man sitting on the porch next door, eating a peach, an out of town early peach, all peachy and juicy. Blue sky, and Artaud says he should have noticed spring sooner. Chaz offers him a beer from his cooler, and everybody joins in when I Heard It Through The Grapevine comes on the boombox.

5. Education. Shakespeare wants to go home, but he also wants a free meal. Spicer is still listening to the radio. Public radio. Poets are on the radio, but they're not saying anything. It's all formalized. They can't grasp the medium, get a sense of the microphone, the audience. "Can't even jerk off right," Spicer mutters. Artaud is chewing a pillow, and then starts to laugh. He turns up the radio, and starts to chant nonsense words back at the poets. Then he calls the station, and asks if anybody know Ode to a Grecian Urn. It starts like this…

6. Initiative. Coltrane again. Dishes pile up in the sink, spaghetti sauce runs down the front of the broken dishwasher.

Through the window, bird songs. Shakespeare is hedging on his promise to wash, instead clowning in an I Hate to Cook apron. "Tomorrow, and tomorrow, and tomorrow…" he says. "I swear it's a fucking comedy." Chaz says he's going home, and offers a ride that Shakespeare jumps at. Good-byes tossed across a version of My Favorite Things. Shakespeare is goofing on Chaz. "Thy nerves are in their infancy again," he says as Chaz starts the truck. "Fuck you, loud-mouth," Chaz replies as they pull away from the curb. We watch them drive off as we take our coffee out on the porch.

7. Staying Power. A warm night. Someplace someone is grilling chicken. Roy Orbison sings down the street. Forsythia glows in the dusk. Artaud wants lilacs. The coffee is strong. Spicer has put a Heart record on the record player. The sky is going to that dark blue on the border of dusk and twilight, and the Wilson sisters are telling the same old story in the same old way and doing it well. The record ends. A night where nothing can go wrong. Narrative time is suspended. Artaud and Spicer are singing Heartbreak Hotel. The improvisation is historic.

8. Passion. I am alone. Spicer has gone home to listen to his own radio. He was quite drunk upon his leave taking. Artaud is going downtown to dance. He is quite drunk and laughing loudly as he goes down the street, lights snapping on in houses as he passes. I hope he doesn't get in a fight. Someone should be at the door, Helen of Troy, or Troy Donahue, but

there's no one. And it's getting late, A knock? I turn on the porch light, but there is no one, not even Linda. You see this isn't really about passion. Only an early moth dancing about a bare light bulb. Someplace someone is playing Bonnie Tyler singing It's a Heartache. I wish I could hear it. I switch off the light and close the door.

=-=

It could almost be summer. It could almost be green. Or maybe the ocean. It could be the ocean. We'll call it the ocean. From a distance the sound of a highway becomes the sound of the surf. The wind along the sand is different from the wind in the trees. A warmer wind in February rattles around in the last stubborn leaves of fall. A cold wind leaves only pain and solitude. The ocean is a lesser blue along the horizon. Even without the ocean there is the thought of the ocean. You find yourself standing at a window. The scarf slides from your shoulder and pools at your feet. A plume of steam rises into the sky and dissipates. A hand on your arm, on your back. A blue jay sits on a bare branch. The mountains are white and a bluish gray. There is a sound like surf through the window. No. There is no sound like surf through the window. There is only the sound of daylight through the window. The sound of cars, of trucks, of a helicopter passing slow along the peak of the roof. A couple is walking down the street. Across the street a cat is watching from under a bush. Another car goes by. The couple watches it pass them. The cat has vanished. Can we even talk about what happens around us without a car battering into our thoughts? Even as you type yes on this page another car passes. Your hat sits on the table. The sun is slipping away. The traffic is thickening out beyond the field, and the mountains are catching the late light, the snow like copper against the bluish gray. Later at night, this is all gone. It is February again, The traffic sounds like surf, becomes the surf, and the tide is going out as you find yourself going on about nothing, about color, about sunlight, about automobiles.

=-=

FROM A KIND OF MOTION WE CALL HEAT

Part 10. "How tedious and timeless the hours." An edited emotion. Is ending a silence a need or a want? The "our" they invoke as they tighten their belts around other's necks. Begin optional trim. A new context: adds and changes should be administered according to a) users, b.) creators, c.) mediators. Ours or hours might depend on the time remaining or perhaps once again possession. It can all come down to a Hail Mary. I wish I could tell the difference between their worlds. What is art? What is commerce? Religion? Competitive sports? Especially since the stories run as long as the days and can often be more interesting. Or would you rather: the day I forgot the sound of your voice. That long pause at the other end of the line. The recollection of the touch of a hand on my arm, an ashtray awash with coffee perched at the end of a table. The details of a woman's walk on July 17th, 1987 as I drove past her heading for Champlain Street, the Northern

Connector and a camp with too many beers as we watched the sun set beyond Mallett's Bay. I'm tired of the old songs, as they say, which is not to say that I don't still listen to them. The sound of a church bell across the hills, or the color of the sky the day someone said goodbye. To discern the distance, or an annotation of the journey? A litany of missed turns and conscious side trips between point A and point B. Can we as residents ever recognize the irony in our own landscapes, the aesthetic potential of these long streams of storefronts when they're finally all empty and abandoned? Begin optional trim. But in the end are my minutiae any more (or less) intriguing than yours? Standard shams. Nattering against this week's list of oppressions, art must always compete for my attention with the moral equivalent of an electric can opener or the lushness of an overgrown garden. A neutral description of the sack of Louvain is neutral how? "How tedious and timeless the hours when Jesus I no longer see. Sweet prospects, sweet birds and sweet flowers, have all lost their sweetness to me." Another language becomes another noise, like this sentence, a clunky kind of communication that starts in the middle of a paragraph with a recounted story, or the mottled sunlight dancing on this page. Begin optional trim.

-=-

THE MONOPOLY OF SORROW

Time, as they say, on your hands. Or to kill. Time to kill. And there is this moment. Or that moment. The divisive moment is the decisive moment. He'd have me call a tree a tree, a rock

a rock, the struggle the struggle. Inventory. A line aligned at a
45 degree angle through a row of arrows. French curves, or
S-curves, the roads out of San Francisco in old movies. Fog
horns, the Golden Gate, that old vocabulary. Pencils. Mechanical pencils. Colored pencils. Or student councils. Long caf-
eteria tables … a fistful of diamonds or a handful of hearts.
Something Mexican then. Chile rellenos or relentless reoccur-
rences. The fog rolls in and rolls off the table. In a certain way,
"thought" meant "nothing." A bell rings. 8 times. It is Sunday.
A talk show on the radio as the alarm goes off by mistake. But
this is a memory. There is no clock radio, just the talk show.
And the bell rings 7 times, not 8. And make that bells, 3 different bells, and that means 21 scattered rings across the city. The
sun runs a pattern through the shades along the wall. A book
is sprawled across a pillow. This is how it works: a voice gets
your attention. It makes you find a pen, a scrap of paper. The
words fall on the table. You have to sort them out. Do you find
your words faster than your thoughts? I do. Another of those
problems peculiar to particular situations. This word is a line,
a road you know. Smoke in the night. Some old song. A vicar-
ious pleasure to be found in the telling, or even in sorting out
these voices. The tone suddenly sharpens. The crimes become
absurd. Supplication, we are suddenly to say. We make up a
situation: a forest, a bed at sunrise, a book sprawled across a
pillow, a body across a curb, as someplace else a car comes to
life, a woman begins to pray, a man to cry. The names fall on
the table. You search for a stub of pencil, a scrap of newspaper.
The light runs along the wall and lands on the sleeping face.

Somebody's singing, "You're burning, baby," and someone else asks, "Hey man, is that your burning baby?"

=-=

When he returned, his memory seemed more like a house abandoned than a house left empty, transformed beyond recognition through neglect and vandalism. Holes smashed through the walls have exposed the interior to the wind, and worse, time. What remained would be of little use to anyone. He resigned himself to reconstruction.

-=-

How would you like to imagine this? Is it like walking in the fog? Or is it more like walking around in a fog? The first day, or a first day (night) by the ocean. When you arrive the tide is coming in and the ocean is out there, halfway down the beach, a minimal pulse of gray surf and sand on a late November afternoon. After dinner, what was left of the sun is long gone, and the murmur of the ocean is now a heavy rolling mumble, as looking out the window, the fog bounces the night off the light above the sill back into your eyes.

=-=

AJAR
The musicians were poised with their instruments. They were ready to go. It would only be a few seconds now, I wrote.
–Richard Brautigan

Or maybe eight jars. I can't remember. C'mon, open 'em. Trust me. Even if it's only one at a time. Love. That's better. That's a start. Now, what do you see? The snow rushing at the windshield, a thin bracelet of taillights running out into the darkness away from you. That's the way to go. Try to remember the old voices. The old faces. All the rest. While we were sitting around the kitchen table solving the problems of the world, the kids were playing in the corner, bombing a building block city with bean bags, a row of pink and blue haired trolls filing away from the holocaust into the living room. Someone is crying. The way a finger traces the line of a chin, the light through a window running down the back. This is a story that is being told someplace else at this very moment, but the odds are that it is being told better. Routing the emotions elsewhere. Another blackness, dressing in the wintry dark, a simple exercise in static electricity recounted three times this week. This time miniature lightning storms cross your legs and flash across your stomach and chest, pushing a dream to the edge of the bed, and off. Before, everything was for sale: another way to start. Street life. Some other silly story of survival. The rivalry of two schools of thought though no one remembers its origins. A revelry gone wrong. Perhaps the wrong person kissed, or missed. The missed person wronged. Or kissed. Perspective. Walking the streets. Rediscovering the buildings, the days. 1962. A party in the next room. The grown-ups. In this room a small photograph sits on a little pedestal of a table in a corner, a bunch of 45s fanned on the floor in front of it. That knocking hiss as you cross the room to lift the tone arm, flip the selector to auto-matic, and now it's the Four Seasons, over and over. The group, not Vivaldi, but I didn't have to tell you that. There's a bookcase with glass doors, and Frankie Valli again and again as you make your way through a shelf of old Thimble Theater cartoon books. That character from the old Popeye stories, what's his name? No, not Wimpy, not Bluto, not Castor Oyl. And all along, "Big girls don't cry, big girls don't cry", and you look around the room. Those high ceilings, that dirty window sill, that dingy anonymous portrait over the fireplace, that door that opens to the stairs leading to the attic store room. This is a room you will dream about again and again when you still remember your dreams, and in thirty years you will read a book by Charles Simic about Joseph Cornell and you will read those lines about miniature theaters and you'll remember this room at the old Sara Holbrook Center on College Street and you will remember the Jeep cavorting with Popeye in an old Thimble Theater omnibus, and you will finally get up and change the record.

-=-

The Way None of This Happened

The tiniest detail matters. It's all a language that you can learn to read. Words, too, can't do more than just evoke things. That's where dance comes in again. –Pina Bausch

The way none of this happened. To want one and write down a gull passing over or through the afternoon, out along the edge of a line of trees and then back across lunchtime as the blue motion of a shadow along the grass. Or to end this silence, write the steady surf-like sound of traffic and the long desperation of brakes sounding down the hill as a solitary bird laughs its sharp tense song at 3 sharps blasts sounding a warning, and a cardinal pokes out bright through the dark green of wet apple leaves at the slight rumble and shudder as the charge is detonated, becoming a jagged red line flashing across the afternoon.

And later the sentence that might change your life is gone, falling back into the pages like a buoy lost below the storm's horizon, and all that can be done for now is to write down the smell of dill on my fingers and the dull orange lip of the day at sunset before a cloudy night.

And later to write down the steady movements of waves onto the shore under the last of the late sunlight settling along the far edge of the field. As a baby starts to cry next door at the sound of hammering echoing across the evening, and gathering darkness makes you look up from your book to see clouds moving in from the north, the wind picking up some stray leaves and tossing their rustles against the water as along the top of a hanging pot of past impatiens, gulls turn a dull pink in all this change.

And still later, with 3 pages left in my notebook, lightning flashes just there on the horizon, and a dog wakes up on the next pier down, rolls to his feet, and starts barking at the following thunder. Two boats racing at us veer south ahead of the oncoming rain, their wakes rocking the piers as another chain of thunder spreads across the lake, and now two guys on seadoos putter past the pier above us into this paragraph in no real hurry, giving me an overheard history of this stretch of South Hero lakefront. Occupations are listed in a who's who and what's where as they approach, and there's that mandatory island nod and wave as they move past me. One last "I dunno but I guess so," and they're off at the next boom of thunder, conversation lost as they accelerate away. Turns out the rain stayed north and now I write down dragonflies dancing across this description of themselves, and my forgotten beer is warm and almost gone along with space for these lines, so that far roll of thunder lends closure to this paragraph, as another line of storms forms up the lake.

Fomite
Burlington, VT

A fomite is a medium capable of transmitting infectious organisms from one individual to another.

"The activity of art is based on the capacity of people to be infected by the feelings of others." Tolstoy, *What Is Art?*

Writing a review on Amazon, Good Reads, Shelfari, Library Thing or other social media sites for readers will help the progress of independent publishing. To submit a review, go to the book page on any of the sites and follow the links for reviews. Books from independent presses rely on reader to reader communications.

For more information or to order any of our books, visit
http://www.fomitepress.com/FOMITE/Our_Books.html

The Moment Before an Injury
Joshua Amses

Nothing Beside Remains
Jaysinh Birjépatil

*The Way None
of This Happened*
Mike Breiner

Victor Rand
David Brizer

Cycling in Plato's Cave
David Cavanagh

Picking Up the Bodies
James F. Connolly

Fomite
Burlington, VT

Unfinished Stories of Girls
Catherine Zobal Dent

Drawing on Life
Mason Drukman

*Foreign Tales of
Exemplum and Woe*
J. C. Ellefson

Free Fall/Caída libre
Tina Escaja

Sinfonia Bulgarica
Zdravka Evtimova

Derail Thie Train Wreck
Daniel Forbes

*Where There Are Two or
More*
Elizabeth Genovise

*The Hundred Yard
Dash Man*
Barry Goldensohn

*When You Remember
Deir Yassin*
R. L. Green

Fomite
Burlington, VT

*A Guide
to the Western Slopes*
Roger Lebovitz

Confessions of a Carnivore
Diane Lefer

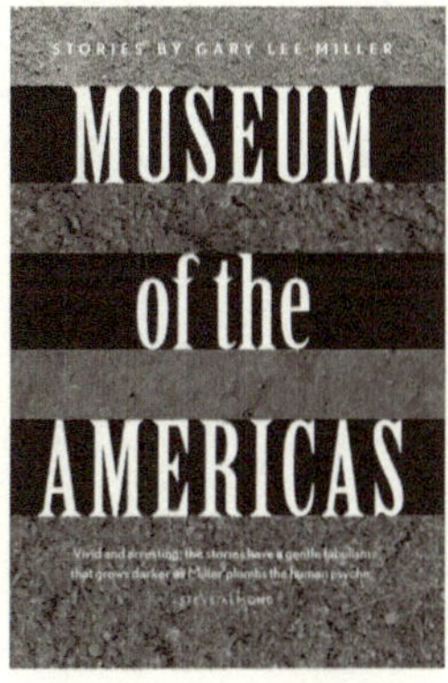

Museum of the Americas
Gary Lee Miller

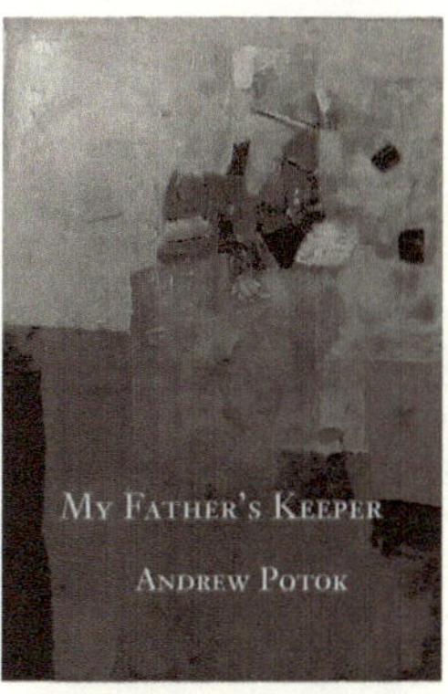

My Father's Keeper
Andrew Potok

*The Hole That Runs
Through Utopia*
Joseph D. Reich

Companion Plants
Kathryn Roberts

Rafi's World
Fred Russell

*My Murder
and Other Local News*
David Schein

Bread & Sentences
Peter Schumann

Fomite
Burlington, VT

Principles of Navigation
Lynn Sloan

Among Angelic Orders
Susan Thoma

Everyone Lives Here
Sharon Webster

The Falkland Quartet
Tony Whedon

*The Return of
Jason Green*
Suzi Wizowaty

*The Inconveniece
of the Wings*
Silas Dent Zobal

Fomite
Burlington, VT

More Titles from Fomite...

Fomite
Burlington, VT

Joseph D. Reich — *The Derivation of Cowboys & Indians*

Joseph D. Reich — *The Housing Market*

Fred Russell — *Rafi's World*

Peter Schumann — *Planet Kasper, Volume 1*

L. E. Smith — *The Consequence of Gesture*

L. E. Smith — *Travers' Inferno*

L. E. Smith — *Views Cost Extra*

Susan Thomas — *The Empty Notebook Interrogates Itself*

Tom Walker — *Signed Confessions*

Susan V. Weiss — *My God, What Have We Done?*

Peter Mathiessen Wheelwright — *As It Is On Earth*

www.ingramcontent.com/pod-product-compliance
Lightning Source LLC
Chambersburg PA
CBHW061452210726
48287CB00007B/2479